HONEY DRAGON

Ashlie Parfitt

First published in Australia in 2024

National Library of Australia Cataloguing-In-Publication data:

Ashlie Parfitt
HONEY DRAGON
ISBNs   978-1-922904-78-2 (paperback)
         978-1-922904-79-9 (eBook)

Cover design by Willsin Rowe

Design, Typesetting & Printing by Clan Destine Press

Chapter 1

LITTLE HUMMINGBIRD.

Small and fragile. Yet, they are brave like the mighty mythological dragons. With their long, slender bill, they gently sip the sweet nectar from the flowers. Their glimmering feathers are impossible to capture on camera as they quickly fly away with their buzzing wings. The sound of their wings can easily be mistaken for a bee.

One tiny hummingbird was brought into the human world. Her majestic hazel eyes were like the hummingbird's feathers when they shine in the sunlight. Her long soft brown hair would flap up and down in the wind like the hummingbird's beating wings.

Kate Summer was her name. But her Uncle Samuel, who raised her, called her Honey Dragon.

"Honey" came from the sweet nectar that the hummingbirds drink while "Dragon" represented their fearless personality, like the mythical beasts themselves.

Even though the pair was used to being stared at wherever they went all, because the two of them were two separate nationalities, Samuel filled Kate's life with laughter and joy.

January 26th, the day before going back to school.

Kate stood in the back yard with her canvas standing in front of her on its wooden frame. Her bowl of paints sat on the pool chair next to her leg while she stroked across the canvas with her paintbrush.

Every few seconds, Kate would peek from behind her canvas to capture the still image of the ocean that slowly danced underneath the hot, smiling sun.

What a wonderful day to paint, Kate thought as she focused on her stroke running across the canvas.

'Heads up!' shouted a voice.

Kate turned her head only to have a shirt thrown at her face.

The shirt dropped onto the grey titles like melted ice cream falling off its cone while Kate heard a loud splashing at the same time.

A few seconds later, Samuel came to the surface. He flicked his black raven, shoulder-length hair and then turned around to find Kate frowning at him. He could tell that steam was coming out of her ears.

'Thanks a lot, muscle god!' said Kate, teasing him with the nickname his female admirers from Night Valley called him, 'you nearly ruined my painting.'

'I said heads up,' Samuel replied as the water dripped down his black goatee and onto his well-muscled chest.

'That is no excuse for nearly ruining my painting.'

'Perhaps I could say the same thing about you calling me muscle god.'

'Perhaps if you were more careful then I wouldn't have to call you muscle god.'

Samuel rolled his eyes and then quickly sank underwater.

Just because you've got millions of dollars and the body of a god doesn't give you the right to throw your shirt at my face, Kate grumbled as she picked up Samuel's shirt from the floor and placed it onto the chair. Her uncle was a history professor and the owner of Night Valley's Museum of History. Despite his wealth, Samuel was determined not to spoil Kate. He was raising Kate like an average fifteen-year-old teenager, although he lived somewhat like an upper-class, forty-three-year-old virgin.

Kate slowly inhaled the warm air into her nose and out of her mouth then, calmed, went back to painting her picture.

After painting for an hour, Kate placed her paintbrush and paint on the chair. Her eyes remained fixed on her half-finished landscape and ignored Samuel as he got out of the pool.

Samuel grabbed his towel from the pool chair and wrapped it around his waist. He then slowly walked over to Kate while the water dripped down his wet legs. He looked over the artist's shoulder at the half-painted landscape of the ocean.

'So, what do you think?' Kate asked Samuel.

Samuel remained silent as he spent a moment analysing the painting.

'I think you're missing a few details,' said Samuel.

'What am I missing?' Kate questioned her uncle.

'The sun and the clouds.'

'I can't paint everything in one day you know.'

'I'm just kidding,' Samuel chuckled as he wrapped his wet arm around Kate.

Kate tried to push herself away from Samuel, but his strong, affectionate grip held her delicate body in a one-armed hug and there was no chance of escaping.

After a while, Samuel released Kate and walked into their modern two-storey house on the hill near the quiet blue ocean, where they lived happily, far away from the rest of the world.

Kate packed up her paints and easel and stored them, along with her new piece, in her studio with her other paintings, which leaned against each other like dominos against the wall.

Back in her room, Kate laid down on her soft bed with her head resting on her pillow. She looked up at the ceiling at her astrological sign: Taurus. The mighty stubborn bull floated in the deep space among the tiny stars in its white constellation form with the outline of the animal itself. She had the ceiling wallpaper custom-made when she was younger as she had always been fond of her animal sign. She had always believed that the bull was the strongest among the other zodiac signs, despite being stubborn and prone to anger.

Closing her eyes, Kate imagined herself riding the strong bull in the night sky filled with crystallised stars at a rapid speed. The other zodiac signs remained frozen and quiet in the empty sky as she and the ghostly bull ran past the giant glowing rock.

'Kate,' Samuel called to her.

Kate opened her eyes. Samuel, dressed in his light blue singlet and black shorts, was smiling at her.

'I was just resting,' said Kate as she sat up and crossed her legs.

Samuel sat down next to Kate on her bed. 'Tomorrow is the start of school, correct?' he said.

'Yes, uncle.'

'I want you to promise me to be a good girl and listen to your teachers.'

'Yes, uncle,' Kate said, rolling her eyes.

'Promise me that you'll stay away from Mr Johnson's daughter.'

'I'll try,' she smiled.

Samuel leaned in and gently kissed Kate's forehead. 'Good girl,' he said then left the room.

'Great!' she grumbled as she dropped her head onto her pillow.

Chapter 2

KATE DIDN'T WANT TO GO BACK TO SCHOOL. SHE WANTED TO STAY in bed and pull the blanket over her face. Instead, she was physically pushed out of the house and into Samuel's blue Ford Mustang. Her heart hammered like it was running in a marathon, and it didn't stop sprinting until the two of them were at Night Valley High.

'Have a nice day at school,' said Samuel.

'Sure.'

Kate grabbed her computer bag and her school bag from the boot before closing the lid.

'I'll see you this afternoon,' Samuel said to Kate as she walked past his car.

If I survive that long, Kate thought as she watched Samuel drive out the front gate.

The young girl sighed as she walked past a giant, overgrown bush that was a few feet taller than she was – only to bump into another student her own age.

'Sorry, Kate,' said the male student as he took his oversized, grey headphones off and placed them around his neck.

'It's alright, Sebastian,' said Kate as he flicked his caramel fringe back from his amber-brown eyes.

Sebastian Wilson had been Kate's childhood friend for as long as she could remember. The two of them did everything together. They had sleepovers together. They drew on the walls with crayons together. They even stole cookies together from the cupboard in Samuel's house.

Sebastian was mostly picked on by other students because of his autistic disorder. As a kid, he was prone to anger and violence and sometimes wouldn't focus on schoolwork. No one knew why these things happened until he was taken to see a specialist. That's when he found out that he was on the spectrum.

After his diagnosis, he started taking medication to control his autism-related anger and saw numerous people to help him with his schooling and managing his autism. Now a teenager, he had learnt to stay away from people who made fun of his condition.

Kate had chosen to remain by his side as his friend instead of leaving him in a deep hole that he couldn't dig out of. She didn't see him as someone with autism but someone who liked wrestling, video games and coding.

'Are you glad to be back at school?' Sebastian asked Kate as the two of them made their way to the lockers.

'Not really,' Kate replied.

'Oh, why?'

'Mary Johnson, remember?'

Sebastian's heart sank to the floor when heard the familiar name.

Mary was known as the bloodsucking leech who loved to feed on people's negative emotions. She had bullied Sebastian ever since she learnt that he was autistic. She especially hated Kate ever since Kate won the school's art competition three years ago. Ever since, she tried to demolish Kate's paintings and tried to drag her underneath the dirt.

The two friends opened their locker doors and placed their school bags inside.

'What do we have first?' Kate asked Sebastian.

'Ancient History,' Sebastian answered as he took off his headphones and placed them into his computer bag then closed his locker door.

Kate closed her locker door only to hear laughter echoing in the corridor. She turned her head and saw a girl walking towards her and Sebastian. The girl had short honey-brown hair that rested a few inches below her ears. Her long fringe covered her left eye. Her entire body was covered in small moles.

'Well, well,' said the girl as she crossed her arms, 'looks like Miss Peasant and Mister Weirdo are still hanging out together.'

'What do you want, Mary?' Kate asked, slinging her computer bag onto her shoulder.

'I want the prize money that you didn't deserve to win three years ago,' Mary said with a cold tone.

Seriously?

'Unlike you, peasant girl, I deserve to have designer bags, clothes and expensive jewellery.'

Kate wished Mary good luck as she and Sebastian walked away from the girl. All the money that she'd won three years ago had been donated to the children's hospitals and towards medical research. Not one cent was left in her pocket.

Sebastian watched as Mary stormed back to her locker.

'Hey Kate,' Sebastian said gently as he looked back at Kate.

'Yes, Sebastian?' said Kate.

'Mary called me a weirdo. Am I a weirdo?'

Kate stopped in front of Sebastian in the middle of the footpath. 'Don't listen to what Mary said about you,' she said.

'But she called me a weirdo.'

'You're not a weirdo. You're my friend and that's all that matters.'

Sebastian smiled at Kate. His smile quickly turned upside down as the bell rang like roaring thunder on a rainy day. He dropped his computer bag onto the hard cement ground and covered his sore ears with his hands.

Kate grabbed Sebastian's bag from the ground. With her other hand, she grabbed Sebastian's uniform shirt and dragged him away from the deafening bell. She didn't let her friend go until the two of them safely arrived at their first class, which was inside a small theatre building standing a few feet away from the music block.

They entered the theatre and sat down in the hard, uncomfortable chairs in the front row, followed by the rest of the class.

A tall, slim man with light blue eyes walked into the building with his computer bag and thick books in his arms. He dropped his items onto the wooden table that stood on the mini stage before adjusting his glasses and fixing his silky, wavy hair.

'Good morning, students.'

'Morning, Mr Winter,' replied the class.

'Before I begin the lesson, I have some good news. I've booked a lesson with Professor Wood at the Museum of History this Friday.'

Sebastian quickly covered his ears with his hands as all the students, except for Kate, cheered like thunder.

Kate rolled her eyes. Her classmates loved to see Samuel Wood whenever they had field trips to the museum. Girls drooled when they saw Samuel's strong arms instead of listening to his words.

When the cheering and the chattering died down, Sebastian lowered his hands and placed them onto his lap.

'I have emailed the permission slip to your parents,' said Mr Winter, 'I expect to have them signed and emailed back before Wednesday.'

Mr Winter wrote on the whiteboard.

The lesson was about Pompeii and Herculaneum, the ancient cities which were engulfed in lava and ash thousands of years ago.

After a long period of listening to Mr Winter's lecture, Kate and Sebastian were glad to get out of their hard chairs to feed their empty stomachs. The two of them casually made their way to their lockers to grab their lunchboxes.

'Hey loser!' a voice shouted.

Kate saw Mary with her arms crossed.

'What do you want now?' Kate asked, ignoring the fire inside Mary's eyes.

'I don't want to see your ugly face when we meet Professor Wood on Friday.'

'And why not?'

'Men like him only talk to beautiful girls and you; you're as ugly as a donkey's ass.'

Kate was at the point of breaking into tears.

'Why don't you do me a favour and go live in a trash can?' Mary said then laughed loudly as she walked away from the friends.

'Are you alright, Kate?' Sebastian asked his friend.

'I'm fine,' Kate answered as she turned her attention back to Sebastian, 'I wish she wasn't such a dodo.'

Sebastian looked puzzled.

Kate clarified that Mary was so stupid that she didn't know that Kate was Samuel's niece.

'Oh.'

The two friends put their bags in their lockers, grabbed their lunchboxes and walked over to the tables. Nearby students laughed and pointed at Kate as she and Sebastian sat down.

'Hey Kate, where did you get your uniform? From the discount shop?' said a male student, making the mob around him laugh loudly.

Kate tried to ignore the hurtful words as she opened her lunchbox and pulled out a small container filled with mouth-watering, juicy red strawberries that Samuel hand-washed with love. She bit into the fruit.

'Why is everyone so mean to you?' Sebastian asked Kate as he ate his peanut butter sandwich.

'I don't know but I wish my uncle would teach them a lesson about not judging people by their appearance,' Kate replied as she took another bite into her strawberry.

'Or what people wear.'

Kate nodded her head. 'Yeah, that too.'

The rest of Kate's first day back at school felt like she was stuck in the middle of the cold ocean surrounded by hungry sharks slowly biting the flesh off her little hummingbird body until there was nothing left.

Kate was glad to leave the nightmarish school. She couldn't handle any more disgusting comments about her appearance and her uniform.

Kate sat in Samuel's car in total silence all the way home. Even then, she didn't speak to Samuel, nor did she look at him.

Samuel watched with worry as Kate dragged her miserable body upstairs to her room. He placed his car keys down onto the dinner table and then walked up the stairs. He walked into Kate's room to find his hummingbird sobbing into her pillow.

'Kate?' Samuel said softly as he gently sat down next to her and placed his hand on her back.

Kate slowly lifted her wet face from her pillow and looked at Samuel with tears flowing down her warm cheeks like a river.

'Why are you crying?' Samuel repeated.

Through her tears, Kate explained. 'Mary said I was ugly. Ugly as a donkey's ass. And the other students laughed at how I dress.'

Samuel covered his open mouth with his hand. His eyes widened in horror. He had never heard such hurtful words in his life. Not only that, the words pierced into Kate's gentle heart like a dart.

'Why does everyone hate me?' Kate sobbed.

'People don't hate you. They are just judgemental,' he said.

'What does that mean?'

'Many years ago, when I opened up the museum, I had many people wanting to work for me. Their resumes were good but most of them did not pass my test.'

'What test?'

Samuel explained that he would dress up and work as a cleaner for a few hours to see if the new candidates would go out of their way to help him out with his job. Most of them treated him like he was nothing more than trash. However, when it was time to do the interview, most of the bullies who treated him poorly, tried to regain his trust when they saw him in a business suit. In the end, only a small handful of people were hired to join his team.

'Like Mary and the rest of the students, karma will come back to bite them in the butt,' Samuel added.

'But how?' Kate asked as she wiped her tears with her hand. 'They'll keep tearing me down.'

'Just wait and see.'

Kate smiled warmly, though her tears continued to flow.

'How do you feel about skipping school for a few days to help me with the presentation for Friday?' said Samuel.

Kate instantly nodded, making Samuel chuckle.

'Well then, we better start researching,' said Samuel, 'but first, why don't you change out of your uniform.'

Samuel left, allowing Kate her privacy. She wiped the remaining tears from her face and then pulled herself off her bed. She pulled out her hair ties, took off her uniform and shoes, and slipped on a plain pink shirt and black pants.

Once dressed, she tied her hair back up then took her dirty clothes into a tall white basket near the washing machine in the laundry and her shoes near the front door.

'What are you learning in ancient history this term?' Samuel asked Kate as he brought his own dirty clothes to the garage. He put them straight into the washing machine.

'Pompeii and Herculaneum.'

'Easy,' Samuel said.

He went into his small library filled with nothing but books about the ancient world. His library, like the garage and the laundry, led off from the first floor.

Kate sat at the dinner table and listened to Samuel pulling out books from his bookshelf and dumping them onto the floor.

Thank goodness I don't have to endure any more pain until Friday, Kate thought.

Kate wondered why so many people at school looked down on her instead of being her friend. She'd told them, countless times, that her uncle was Samuel Wood. Nobody believed her.

Her teachers knew that Kate was Samuel's niece, but none of her classmates had ever seen him drop her at school. They only thought of Professor Wood as a rich, handsome, single man and somehow that meant he couldn't possibly be related to her.

Her classmates weren't the only ones who treated them like they were strangers to each other rather than family – all because Kate and Samuel didn't look much alike. Samuel was born in Japan of Japanese parents while fair-skinned Kate was born in Night Valley, Australia.

Kate once asked to learn to read and speak her uncle's language but ultimately gave up as she didn't have the patience and time to listen to her uncle. So, whenever they went to Japan, she got her uncle to translate everything.

A few minutes later, Samuel walked out of his library his arms full of books. He dumped the books onto the dinner table and then sat down next to Kate.

'How many books did you grab?' Kate asked, looking at the pile.

'Just a few. I've got loads more in my office at the museum,' Samuel answered. He grabbed the first book from the pile and opened it to the first page.

Kate pretended to listen to Samuel as he talked about the eruption that buried the ancient cities Pompeii and Herculaneum thousands of years ago, even though she already knew about the famous volcano.

Kate was finally freed from Samuel's history lesson. By the time the clock struck six, she had showered and was at the dinner table in her pyjamas, eating her freshly cooked vegetables with Samuel. Rather than hire staff to cook and clean, Samuel enjoyed cooking for them both. The pair cleaned the house every weekend together.

'Are you alright now?' Samuel asked Kate as he ate his broccoli.

'Not really,' Kate answered, 'I'm still upset about today.'

'Don't worry, Honey Dragon, you just have to wait patiently.'

'I hope that I don't have to wait too long.'

'Me too, Honey Dragon.'

Chapter 3

THE FIRST DAY OF SCHOOL HAD STARTED ON THE WRONG FOOT FOR Kate. She was thankful that she didn't have to spend another day enduring more pain from Mary and the other students.

Helping out Samuel with his museum was more exciting and fun than sitting in a classroom and being forced to do schoolwork.

The next day, the two of them casually walked inside the large museum to find an endless crowd of people on various floors. Their laughter and chatter could be heard throughout the museum.

Kate's heart sped up as she and Samuel walked through the mob. Their leering eyes followed them across the room while she heard some of the women whisper about Samuel using his well-earned salary on an adopted young girl like her, rather than getting married and having children of his own.

As much as the comments were hurtful like darts, Kate ignored the women. She couldn't understand why so many people treated her like she was an outcast while everyone tried to sweep Samuel off his feet.

Why do we live in a judgemental society? Kate thought as she followed Samuel into his office.

Samuel's office was taller and wider than his employees' offices. His wall was full of shelves with endless rows of books. Not a single book was out of place. His desk stood in the middle of the room with a photo of him and Kate from when they travelled to Japan during its winter season. A smaller table stood against the wall was filled with important paperwork.

'I'm sorry about the mess,' Samuel said as he placed his bag onto his desk then grabbed the heavy files from the other table and placed them onto the floor.

'Why don't you ever put your work in the filing cabinet?' Kate asked as she looked at the cabinet that was standing centimetres away.

'I'm constantly busy doing reports and other important work,' Samuel answered.

'You mean the single ladies are keeping you busy with the phone calls.'

'Don't be silly,' he complained as he dropped the remaining files onto the floor.

Kate giggled while Samuel blushed.

Samuel crossed his arms. 'I don't associate with women who are after my money and status rather than my heart.'

Samuel's desk phone rang loudly.

Samuel inhaled through his nose and then out of his mouth before picking up the phone.

'Hello. This is Professor Wood from the Museum of History; how may I help you?'

Kate sat at the table and placed her phone on it.

'No!' Samuel shouted, making Kate look back at him. 'No! I'm not selling my museum anytime soon. Good day!'

With that, Samuel furiously hung up. 'Bastard,' he grumbled.

'Was that Mr Johnson?' Kate asked.

'Yes.'

Kate rolled her eyes as she opened her bag.

'Why would that idiot want to buy the museum when he already owns five casinos?' Kate unpacked her art diary and her pencil case. Kate's diary was fully black. The cover had a white, plain symbol of her zodiac sign.

'I don't know either, but he will never turn this museum of wonder into a gambling monstrosity.'

Knock! Knock!

A man wearing a grey business suit and a black necktie walked into the room. His eyes and hair were the same colour as Sebastian's. His long, grey-streaked hair was tied up in a bun. Even his stubbly beard had a streak of grey hair running through it.

'Morning boss,' the man joked.

'Jake, you know you can just call me Samuel,' said Samuel.

'I know, I know, but it's not professional if I call you by your first name.'

'We're friends you know.'

'I know,' Jake said as he turned his attention towards Kate. 'Hello, Kate.'

'Hello, Jake,' said Kate.

'May I ask why you aren't at school?'

Kate quickly turned her head away from Jake as she crossed her arms.

Samuel told Jake about Mary's hurtful comments.

Jake wasn't surprised. Mary had the same attitude as her father, Mr Johnson. They were like snakes who loved to bite innocent people with their razor-sharp fangs and inject them with their poison. Neither of them gave up until their prey no longer had the strength to breathe.

'Speaking of Mary, I was just on the phone with her father,' said Samuel.

'Seriously?' Jake grumbled, 'Is he still trying to convince you to sell the museum?'

'Yes.'

Buzz! Buzz!

Samuel pulled out his vibrating phone from the pocket in his shirt and answered the call.

Jake casually walked over to Kate while Samuel walked out of his office and closed the door behind him.

'I wish Mary would stop bullying you,' said Jake.

'Me too,' Kate responded as she pulled her lunch box from her bag and placed it down next to her art diary on the table.

'Well, at least she won't hurt you today.'

'She won't be hurting me until next week.'

'What do you mean?' Jake asked with his eyebrow raised.

Kate explained to Jake that she was skipping a few days of school to help out Samuel with Friday's presentation for Ancient History class.

Jake smiled, knowing that Kate was a lucky girl to have a special man like Samuel in her life.

A few minutes later, Samuel walked back into his office.

'Who was that on the phone?' Kate wanted to know.

'It was Mr Winter,' Samuel answered. 'He was worried about you.'

'What did you say to him?'

'I said you were helping me out with the presentation for Friday and can't attend school until next week,' he said. He walked over to his desk and logged into his computer.

Once Samuel was in his computer, he asked Jake to take his and Kate's lunch to the staff room and put them in the fridge. Jake cheerfully collected their lunches and left the office, only to stop in the middle of the doorway.

'I was wondering if you want to hit the bar this Sunday with me,' said Jake.

'Jake, you know how I feel about leaving Kate alone,' Samuel responded.

'Come on, man! She's fifteen years old. I'm sure she'll be fine with Sebastian for a few hours.'

Samuel shook his head.

'Come on! That cobra isn't going to bite Kate anytime soon.'

Samuel walked over to his friend and pulled him out of his office then slammed the door behind him, leaving Kate alone in the soundless office.

That...was weird, Kate thought as she settled at her table.

Kate opened her art diary to a page with a half-sketched drawing of a fox sleeping peacefully on the grass. She then selected her pencil and continued to sketch the animal without thinking too much about what Jake just said.

After some time, Samuel returned to his office.

'That man doesn't know when to shut up,' he said.

'You know how Jake is,' Kate replied. 'He loves to talk and talk.'

Samuel looked at the fine details of the sleeping fox she'd drawn, impressed. The shades and texture made the animal look realistic in its environment.

'How cute,' he said.

'Do you like it?' Kate asked.

'I do, except you're missing something.'

'And what's that?'

'Colour.'

'I need to draw the rest of the background before I can add colour.'

Samuel smiled and then walked to his desk to begin his work.

'Hey uncle,' said Kate.

'Yes, Kate?' Samuel replied as he began to type on his keyboard.

'Thanks again for taking me out of school for a few days.'

'Anytime, Honey Dragon.'

Samuel clicked on his PowerPoint software and began to type.

Kate quietly got up from her chair and walked up behind Samuel. She watched as the words poured onto the screen. Her eyes could barely keep up with Samuel's speed as he continued to write in another next box.

'This presentation will be done in a few hours,' said Kate.

'The presentation doesn't stop there,' said Samuel. 'I still have to edit it and source the information.'

'Oh, right. I almost forgot about that.'

Samuel went back to typing only to stop when he heard someone softly knocking on his door. A tall man with short, sandy hair walked into the room. He wore a plain white shirt with a security guard badge attached and long black pants. Attached to his belt were his handheld radio and his gun. A small red scar sliced through the man's left eyebrow like a cat's claw mark.

'Good morning, Professor Wood, and good morning, Miss Summer,' said the man with a smile on his face.

'Morning, Shawn,' said Samuel, 'how can I help you?'

'Alex asked me to tell you that she received a phone call from an anonymous woman who requests to speak to you.'

'Can't Alex put the call through to my phone instead?'

Shawn shook his head. 'Unfortunately, no.'

'Kate, can you edit the presentation while I go answer this call?' Samuel asked as he rose.

'Of course, uncle,' said Kate as she took Samuel's chair.

Samuel asked Shawn to keep his eyes on Kate before leaving.

'I see that you're not at school today,' said Shawn.

'I know, but it's not my fault,' Kate replied. 'Mary is to blame.'

'Is she still bullying you because you won the art competition three years ago?'

Kate nodded her head and then turned her attention towards the screen. She quietly read each box while fixing the words that Samuel misspelled.

After ten minutes of constant editing, Kate dropped her head onto Samuel's desk.

'Are you alright, Miss Summer?' Shawn asked.

'I'm alright,' Kate responded as she looked up at the man. 'This presentation, on the other hand, hurts my brain.'

Shawn let out a chuckle. 'You're not used to your uncle's job.'

Kate wondered how her uncle could write and do so many presentations without putting stress on his brain, and still manage to put a smile on his face every day. She got up from Samuel's desk and went back to the smaller table to work on her sketch.

Samuel returned to find Shawn standing next to his desk, watching the young girl who had her head down with her eyes fixed on her picture. Her hand didn't move the pencil off the paper.

'How's the young artist going?' Samuel asked Shawn.

'She's fine,' Shawn answered, turning towards Samuel. 'She has not moved from her chair.'

'I'm not surprised. She doesn't move whenever she's deep into her drawing or painting.'

'Well,' Shawn said, 'I better get going.'

Samuel thanked Shawn as the man left. He waited until the door was closed then walked over to Kate and placed his hand onto her shoulder.

Kate placed her pencil down next to her diary and then twisted in her chair to look up at Samuel. 'Oh, you're back already,' she said.

'I don't mess around when I answer calls,' Samuel replied.

'So...who rang you?'

'No one special.'

Kate lowered her eyes towards the small bump in Samuel's suit. 'What's that in your pocket?'

'I got a surprise for you,' said Samuel as he pulled out a small square box from his pants.

'What is it?'

Samuel opened the lid to reveal a silver pendant that was shaped like a hummingbird. Its wings were filled with tiny cerise and orchid-coloured gemstones that sparkled underneath the light. Even its little body was filled with orchid stones. A single black gemstone acted as the bird's eye.

'It's beautiful,' said Kate as Samuel gently took the necklace out of its box. 'But hang on. I thought you said you would never spoil me with gifts?'

'Well,' Samuel replied as he unhooked the necklace and placed it around Kate's neck. 'I got this gift to remind you how much I love you.'

Kate got up and wrapped her arms around Samuel. 'I promise to never lose this necklace.'

Samuel hugged Kate back and kissed her forehead.

'So...uhh...what happens now that you're finished with the presentation?' Kate asked Samuel.

'I still have to do a bit of editing,' Samuel responded. 'After that, we can do whatever we want until Friday.'

'Don't you need to be at the museum to make sure everything is in place?'

Samuel shook his head. 'If there's a problem, someone will ring me,' he said.

He returned to his desk and Kate sat back at hers to continue with her drawing without stopping to check the time on her phone.

After some time, Samuel turned his attention to the time in the corner of his screen.

'12:15,' he said out loud. 'Man, time does fly. Are you hungry?'

He never got a response. He walked over to Kate to find her eyes frozen on her picture while the tip of the pencil continued to run back and forth across the page.

'Kate,' said Samuel.

Kate paid no attention to Samuel as she focused on her drawing.

'Hey!' Samuel clicked his fingers in front of Kate's eyes until he finally gained her attention.

'What do you want, uncle?' Kate asked Samuel grouchily.

'Aren't you hungry?'

Kate placed her pencil down and checked the time on her phone. '12:16,' she said. 'Why didn't you tell me it was lunchtime?'

Samuel wanted to slap his forehead but instead rolled his eyes. 'Let's go,' he said. 'We're having lunch then we'll be leaving.'

Kate followed Samuel out of his office. She remained close to him as they made their way up to the third level.

At the top floor, a group of security guards greeted Samuel and Kate as the two of them walked into the lunch room. Most of the employees were sitting down at the table with food in their mouths while their eyes were glued onto their phones.

'Hey guys!' said Jake as he pulled out his lunch from the microwave. 'I got your food out already.'

'Thanks, Jake,' said Samuel.

Kate and Samuel walked over to the table where their lunchboxes were and sat beside each other.

Jake joined them with his own lunch. 'How's that presentation coming along?' he asked.

'That's done and dusted,' Samuel answered.

Jake wasn't surprised. His friend knew most of the ancient world like the back of his hand.

The two older men chattered away. Kate quietly listened to their conversation while eating her strawberry jam sandwich.

After everyone's stomachs were full of food, the employees made their way back to their desks. Kate returned with Samuel to his office to pack up their belongings.

'What are we going to do until Friday?' Kate asked Samuel as she placed her diary, pencil case and lunchbox into her bag.

'For starters, I want to show you something tomorrow that you might love,' Samuel answered as he logged off his computer.

'Oh? What is it?'

'You'll find out tomorrow.'

Knock! Knock!

Samuel and Kate turned their heads towards the door to find a woman with fair skin and cute brown eyes slowly walking into the office, a pile of envelopes in her hands. Her short black hair tickled the top of her shoulders like tiny little hands. Two silver rods dangled from the woman's ears. Attached to the rods were tiny flowers with lime green gemstone petals that glimmered in the light. She wore a plain white shirt under her black skirt suit.

The woman bowed her head as she greeted Samuel and Kate in Japanese.

'Ah, Alex,' Samuel said, and spoke to the woman in Japanese as he walked up to her.

Alex, another history professor, was one of the museum's conservators. She often liked to help Samuel out with his presentations and occasionally brought his mail.

Kate stood quietly in her spot as she listened to Samuel and Alex chattering away in Japanese even though she couldn't understand a single word.

I wish I understood what they were saying, Kate thought as she grabbed her phone from the table. She looked at several photos of different landscapes, noting new ideas for her next project.

After several minutes of talking, Alex handed Samuel the pile of envelopes and then bowed her head. 'Enjoy the rest of the day with Kate,' she said, then left with a huge smile on her face.

'What did you two talk about?' Kate asked as she placed her phone into her pocket.

'Oh, just boring work stuff,' Samuel answered in English.

'Like those envelopes in your hand?'

'Yeah. Nothing exciting about that.'

'What's this thing you need to show me tomorrow?' Kate wanted to know, changing the subject.

Instead of answering Kate, Samuel smiled. 'Wait patiently until tomorrow.'

Kate never stopped flapping her little wings whenever Samuel planned surprises for her. She would flood him with a million questions but never receive a single answer until she saw the surprise for herself.

I hate waiting, Kate grumbled.

Chapter 4

THE NEXT MORNING, KATE WALKED INTO SAMUEL'S UPPER-FLOOR bedroom to find him putting away his clean laundry. She sat down on the side of his bed.

'So,' she said, 'what's this thing you need to show me?'

'Are you still going on about that?' said Samuel with a huge smile on his face.

'I will not shut up until you show me.'

Samuel handed Kate a pile of her clean clothes from the washing basket. 'Put your clothes away, then I might tell you.'

Kate instantly sprinted out of Samuel's room juggling the pile of clothes in her arms and into her own room that was next door to Samuel's room.

Samuel returned the empty basket to the downstairs laundry. When he walked back into the house, he heard Kate's voice above him.

'So, are you going to tell me now?'

Samuel looked up and saw Kate leaning against the railing of their home's interior bridge, which stretched between the bedrooms and bathrooms on one side of the second storey to the art studio, office and storage room on the other.

'Yes, uncle,' Kate replied, smiling down at him.

'Are you sure?'

'Yes!'

'Well then. Let's get going.'

Kate sprinted across the bridge and down the stairs. She zoomed passed him like a hummingbird flying away from a large predator and disappeared into the garage.

'I wish she moved that fast on school days,' he said as he grabbed his keys, phone and wallet from the dinner table and then joined her, locking the door after him.

In the car, Kate asked again. 'Can I at least have a clue?'

'If I tell you, it won't be a surprise.'

'Please.'

'No.'

Seatbelts on, Samuel opened the roller door with a press of a button on his keychain, pulled out into the driveway, closed the garage and then drove away.

Kate grabbed Samuel's phone from the cupholder and went into his music app.

'What are you doing?'

'Playing some music,' Kate answered.

'Please no! Whatever you do, do not play that music.'

Kate smirked at Samuel and pressed play for her music list, which she snuck onto Samuel's phone in case she wanted to torture him with her favourite artist.

When he heard Two Steps from Hell playing, Samuel wanted to scream, or jump out of the car. But he couldn't. He was forced to listen to what Kate described as heavenly music.

Each song on the album represented different human emotions that depended on the different instruments, such as bass drum and string instruments. Some songs were sung by a woman, others had a male lead singer, and some had both.

'Now this is good quality music,' said Kate.

'Good quality music? I rather listen to my own music,' Samuel replied.

'Yeah, in a language that I don't understand.'

'Exactly! So that I can sing without you having to know the lyrics.'

In that moment, Kate remembered that when was younger, she walked into Samuel's room to find him singing to one of his favourite Japanese movies. His singing voice sounded like it could break a mirror.

'Maybe we should just stick to listening to my music,' said Kate.

'Perhaps next time, I should sing a few of my songs,' Samuel replied.

'No thanks, uncle.'

Kate then turned her attention towards the window. *Man! If he sings, I'm moving to another country.*

As they listened, Kate looked out the window at the massive trees with branches that touched each other. Their green leaves were like hands holding the sun like a delicate flower in their palms.

What a beautiful sight, Kate thought.

Samuel glanced at Kate then pressed the pause button on the screen with his finger.

'Hey!' Kate protested. 'I was listening to that!'

'We're here,' said Samuel.

Kate gasped when she saw the name engraved on the dark green wooden sign. 'No way!' she said with excitement. 'Night Mountain.'

'See, what did I tell you?' he said. 'If I told you, it wouldn't have been a surprise.'

'I can see why now.'

Samuel drove along the dirt road until he finally found an empty spot on the grass to park.

'I wonder how many of your feathered friends we'll see today,' Samuel joked as he turned off the engine.

'That was not funny,' Kate replied then got out of Samuel's car.

Samuel got out, locked his vehicle and followed Kate. He paid no attention to the crowd of people whispering about him as he and Kate passed them.

'You've got people whispering about you again,' said Kate, overhearing the people behind her.

'I know, I know,' Samuel responded, 'just ignore them.'

Kate let out a soft sigh as Samuel wrapped his arm around her.

'Cheer up Honey Dragon, we're here to see your friends, remember.'

'Yes uncle,' she said in a low tone as she lowered her head.

Kate watched her feet moving along the grass. She only looked up when she heard a kookaburra.

In front of Samuel and Kate stood a giant eucalyptus tree. Its branches and leaves touched the sky. Sitting among the many branches was the laughing kookaburra. One of Night Valley's native birds.

'There's one of your friends,' said Samuel, rubbing the side of Kate's arm with his hand.

Finding the touch distracting, Kate pulled Samuel's hand off her arm while not taking her eyes off the laughing bird. 'Kookaburras are cool, but I prefer my other friends.'

Pointing towards the lower branches of the tree, Samuel spotted two birds that looked like every colour of the rainbow was painted on their tiny bodies. Their backs were covered in green feathers while their faces were the same colour as the ocean. They were happily eating away the tiny red thorn-like flowers.

Kate gasped with surprise when she saw the two moving rainbows.

'Oh my gosh! The lorikeets are so cute,' she said as her cheeks glowed.

'They're cute but they're not as cute as a hummingbird,' said Samuel.

That made Kate thoughtful. 'Out of all the birds in the world, why was I nicknamed after a hummingbird?' she asked.

Samuel was about to explain when someone tapped on his shoulder. He and Kate turned around to find a woman staring at him. She was older than Samuel, and she had two different coloured eyes. One was blue. One was green. Her short, copper-red, curly hair barely touched the tip of her shoulders and what Kate could see of her skin was covered in tiny moles. She wore a plain black shirt, cut away at her shoulders. Her blue-coloured jeans matched her slip-on shoes.

'Good morning, professor,' said the woman in a friendly tone.

'Good morning, uhh…' replied Samuel.

'Samantha.'

'May I ask why you tapped on my shoulder, Samantha?'

'I was just wondering if you were getting paid to babysit this teenager.'

'Excuse me?!' Kate demanded.

'I am spending time with my niece,' Samuel clarified stiffly.

Samantha instantly burst into laughter. 'Niece?' she chuckled. 'You are funny, professor.'

'I'm serious. This teenager is my niece, and I'm her guardian.'

'Oh please. Single men aren't guardians to children.'

'This one is.'

Samantha wasn't put off. 'You should have a wife and your own children, you know, instead of taking care of someone else's.'

Samuel's eyes burned like a flame slowly melting the candle wax. He clenched his teeth.

'Listen here, lady!' snapped Samuel, 'I'm happy being single and raising a teenager. I don't need another woman in my life. I especially don't need a woman who treats me and Kate differently. Got it?!'

Samantha, startled, quickly nodded her head.

'So go away, move on with your life, and never bother us again.'

Samantha hurried away, got into her small blue car and drove away.

'Are you alright, uncle?' Kate asked Samuel, noticing that his eyes were shining with tears.

'Y-yes,' Samuel wiped his tears away.

'Are you sure? You looked like you were about to cry.'

'I said yes!'

Samuel's sudden volume nearly made Kate break out in tears too. Her ears rang like a bell for several seconds. Her warm heart felt like it was sliced in half.

'Oh my gosh,' said Samuel as he tightly wrapped his arms around the shaken Kate, 'I'm so sorry. I didn't mean to shout at you. I'm just...always pestered by people wanting me to settle down and have kids. Women offer drinks so they can try and win my heart. I declined them all.'

'I'm sorry you went through that,' Kate said with a soft tone.

'It's alright,' Samuel replied as he rubbed Kate's back with his hands. 'I'm just happy to have a niece like you in my life.'

'I'm happy to have you as my uncle.'

Samuel smiled for a brief second then let out a soft sigh. 'I'm sorry again for shouting at you.'

'It's alright.'

Samuel released Kate. 'Do you want ice-cream?'

Kate instantly nodded her head at the mention of one of her favourite foods in the world.

Samuel grinned as he watched the young girl sprinting back to his car.

Thank goodness her little hummingbird spirit forgave me, Samuel thought.

By the time he returned to his car, Kate was already waiting for him to unlock the vehicle.

'Come on!' said Kate as she jumped up and down like a child who had too much sugar in their system. 'I want some ice cream.'

'Perhaps next time I shouldn't mention your favourite food,' he said as they got into the car.

'Can we go to that small café near the waterfall?'

'I have a better idea.'

'It better not be one of your surprises.'

Samuel said nothing as he drove past the gigantic tree and Kate's feathered friends.

The pair soon arrived at a large café where the trees towered above the building in the background like mountains.

'Night Mountain Café,' Kate said, reading the gigantic sign on the building. 'I've never heard of this place.'

'You have now.'

Samuel parked and they walked inside. People were gathered around the many tables, happily chattering and laughing whilst enjoying their meals underneath the large ceiling fans.

Samuel and Kate sat at one of the tables.

Kate's jaw nearly dropped to the floor when she saw the paintings on the wall of all the types of bird species that lived in Night Valley hanging on the wall. She saw kookaburras, lorikeets, ducks and other colourful and unique birds.

'Night Valley is a lucky place to have such beautiful species of birds,' Kate said.

She's just like her mother, Samuel thought as he smiled at Kate.

'Samuel,' called a voice.

Samuel turned his head and saw a waiter approaching their table with menus in his arms. He wore a black apron over his plain white shirt. His short brown hair stood up on the top of his head like spikes. His face showed not one single facial hair growing. Wrapping around the man's right arm was a tattoo of a snake.

'Hey Carl,' said Samuel. Samuel had met Carl while studying for his bachelor's degree in business.

'What can I get you and the young artist on this fine day?' Carl asked Samuel as he placed the menus on the table.

'I'll just have an espresso,' Samuel requested.

'And what about the artist?'

'Vanilla ice cream with sprinkles.'

'Does she want a drink with that?'

Kate paid no attention; she continued to admire the paintings on the wall.

'Kate,' said Samuel, waving his hand in front of Kate's face. 'Hello.'

'Huh?'

'Would you like a drink with your ice cream?'

'Just water.'

'Excellent,' said Carl, jotting down the order and taking back the menus. 'I'll see you guys soon.'

With that, Carl left Samuel and Kate alone.

Samuel grabbed his phone from his pocket and immediately grumbled.

'Is everything alright?' Kate asked.

'I'm fine,' Samuel replied, 'just gotta read an endless list of emails when we get home.'

Kate yanked the phone out of his hand.

'Hey!' he complained, 'what was that for?'

Kate turned off his phone. 'Can't you go one day without thinking about work?'

'Kate, you know I get a million calls if I don't answer my emails.'

Kate placed his phone into her pocket and then turned her attention back towards the paintings.

Definitely takes after her mother.

Carl soon returned to Samuel and Kate's table with a tray.

'Here you go, Samuel,' he said as he carefully placed the hot cup of coffee, a bowl of ice cream and a glass of water onto the table.

Kate immediately grabbed her spoon and dug into her ice cream like she was flying around from flower to flower, tasting the ever-sweet, mouth-watering nectar.

'How's your business going?' Samuel asked Carl then took a small sip from his cup.

'Business is going well,' Carl responded as he sat down next to Samuel with the tray pressed against his chest. 'I've actually expanded the café.'

'Wow! Congratulations.'

'Thanks, man.'

While the two men were busy chattering and laughing, Kate pulled out her phone and, looked up different coloured roses on the internet. Well, she mostly looked up pink, purple, red and white roses.

Carl looked at Kate for a few seconds then back at Samuel. 'How's your life with an artist going?'

'Don't get me started on that,' said Samuel then took another sip. 'She hates it whenever I interrupt her or try to sabotage her paintings.'

Carl let out a soft chuckle. 'At least you have a teenager to keep you company.'

'True.'

'Is you-know-who back yet?' he asked, changing the subject.

Samuel leaned closer to Carl. 'No, she isn't,' he whispered. 'And it's best not to talk about her in front of Kate, got it?'

Carl nodded.

After the long conversation, Samuel paid and said goodbye to Carl before leaving.

'Thanks for the ice cream, uncle,' said Kate.

'Anytime, Honey Dragon,' Samuel replied. He pressed a button on his keychain which opened the car and Kate sprinted ahead to the car and jump into her seat.

Samuel was about to open his car door when he suddenly heard a man shouting his name. A gigantic man was walking up to him. Samantha stood several feet away from him with her arms crossed.

The man was as muscular as Samuel. Both of his arms were covered in tattoos of terrifying human skulls that would make anyone quake in fear.

Samuel felt like a tiny mouse looking up at the man – and he was six foot two. 'Can I help you?'

Samuel was suddenly yanked by his shirt towards the man's boiling red face.

'How dare you threaten my girlfriend!' yelled the man.

'W-what are you talking about?' said Samuel with confusion.

'Don't play dumb with me! Samantha told me that you threatened her.'

'I would never threaten a woman. Ever.'

The man pulled his other arm back and clenched his rock-hard fist.

'Stop!' cried Kate.

The man looked away from Samuel and saw the young teenager running up to him with tears pouring from her eyes.

'Don't you dare hurt my uncle!' Kate roared.

'Or what?' said the man with a cold voice.

'Or...or I'll call the police.'

'Whatever,' the man grumbled, but he dropped Samuel.

Kate ran up to Samuel and tightly wrapped her arms around him. She dropped her head onto his chest and wept floods of tears. She felt his arms wrapping around her body but paid no attention to him rubbing her back.

'Let's go, sugar,' said the stranger as he took Samantha's hand.

Samuel remained quiet as he watched the couple wander off down the road out of sight.

'Thank goodness. They're gone,' he said then turned his attention towards Kate. 'Are you alright, Honey Dragon?'

Kate continued to cry. 'No,' she responded, 'I...I...'

Samuel gently rubbed her tears with his thumb. 'Let's go home.'

Kate slowly nodded and then made her way back to her seat.

As he began the drive home, Samuel saw that tears still streamed down her face while she stared at the floor. She held her seatbelt against her chest while her fingers stroked it like she was stroking an animal.

Poor thing, Samuel thought as he drove off, *that hawk must've scared off her feathers.*

Kate lay on her bed with a stuffed red panda, her arms wrapped around its soft body. Her fingers slowly ran through its fur.

Samuel opened Kate's bedroom door to find her still swimming in her tears. He walked into her room and sat down on the edge of her bed.

'Kate?' he said with a gentle voice.

Kate slowly opened her wet eyes.

'Are you alright?'

Kate quickly turned her head away.

'If something is troubling you, you can tell me.'

'It's... It's about the man we met earlier.'

'Oh...him.'

Kate wiped the tears from her eyes and then sat up, her panda still resting against her chest. She swung her legs over the side of her bed and rested her head against Samuel's arm.

'That man,' Kate sobbed, staring at the floor, 'he looked like one of those scary predatory birds.'

'That's one way of describing him,' Samuel replied.

'When I saw his fist, I thought he was going to punch you until there was nothing left of your face.'

Samuel placed his hand underneath Kate's chin and gently turned her head until she was looking up at him.

'That man would've punched my face if your little hummingbird spirit hadn't stopped him,' he said. 'Thank you for protecting me.'

'You're welcome,' said Kate, smiling at last.

'Now, who's up for a swim?'

'Yes, please.'

'I'll see you in the pool,' he said and then left.

Once Kate was dressed in her swimmers, she made her way into the backyard where she found Samuel standing near the edge of the pool looking out onto the ocean.

This man is taking too long, Kate thought as she slowly walked up behind Samuel and shoved him into the pool.

'What the heck, Kate!' said Samuel as he flicked his hair back. 'Why did you push me?'

'You were taking too long,' Kate replied.

'I was literally standing there for a minute.'

Kate rolled her eyes and then jumped into the water.

'Perhaps next time I should push you into the pool,' said Samuel.

'You won't dare do that to your little hummingbird.'

Samuel crossed his arms and looked at Kate with red cheeks while she looked at him with a huge smirk on her face.

'Anyway,' said Samuel. 'I'll be busy tomorrow paying bills. Try not to disturb me, okay?'

'Yes, uncle.'

Chapter 5

THE FOLLOWING DAY, SAMUEL WAS IN HIS OFFICE, NEXT DOOR TO Kate's studio, opening envelopes. Most of the mail was bills, which was nothing new to Samuel.

'Why bills?' Samuel grumbled, 'why couldn't I get something more exciting than bills?'

He dropped them next to his computer and then rubbed his eyes.

A few seconds later, a hand touching his shoulder. Kate was standing beside him with several envelopes in her hands.

'Are you alright, uncle?' Kate asked.

'Yeah. Just gotta pay the bills as usual for the museum,' Samuel answered.

'Well, I hate to break to you, but you've got more bills to pay.'

Samuel slapped his forehead. 'Thanks.'

Kate placed the new mail on his desk and then went into her studio.

Samuel sat back in his chair and read the list of bills out loud as he dropped them onto his desk. He halted when he held the last envelope in his hand.

On the front of it, Samuel's full name was written in black ink in a cursive font. On the back, the seal was taped down by a red love heart sticker.

Curious, Samuel opened the envelope, pulled out the letter and then unfolded it. He read it then suddenly, with fire in his eyes, crushed the letter into a tight ball and threw it into the bin underneath his desk.

'There is no way that vulture is coming back!' Samuel roared.

Samuel punched his desk, but the fire inside only grew hotter and brighter to the point that tears ran down his cheeks.

'Is everything alright in here?' Kate asked as she entered Samuel's office.

'Stupid bird!' Samuel roared.

Startled, Kate immediately backed away from Samuel with her ears ringing. She started to cry. The gentle flame that warmed her heart was blown out by a gush of wind.

'Oh my gosh,' said Samuel when he realised that his voice had shaken every single feather off Kate's body. He tried to apologise, but she sprinted out of his office in more tears. 'What have I done?'

Samuel rushed into Kate's room. He found her face in her pillow, sobbing.

'Kate?' Samuel softly stroked her spine. 'I'm sorry.'

'If you're sorry,' she sobbed, 'why did you call me a stupid bird?'

'I didn't mean you. I got a letter from my ex-girlfriend saying that she wants to get back together with me again.'

Never in Kate's life did she expect to hear the word "ex-girlfriend" coming out of Samuel's mouth. 'You...you had a girlfriend?'

'Yes, many years ago.'

'You never told me that you had one.'

'That's because she stabbed me in the back.'

'How?'

'I'm sorry but that's something I cannot share with you.'

Kate wiped her tears and then rolled over on the damp pillow. 'Was she like the Taurus bull?'

No,' he said, 'she was more like a thorn disguised as a hummingbird.'

'You mean a stupid bird?'

'Yeah...exactly. I never meant to call you a...a stupid bird,' said Samuel, ashamed his outburst had hurt her. 'I know I've raised a beautiful bird with a warm and creative heart. And I know my apology might not be enough, but can you find it in your heart to forgive me?'

'Not until you deal with Mary tomorrow,' said Kate.

'I will. Don't you worry.'

'What are you going to do about your ex?'

'Nothing,' he said as he got up.

'Nothing?'

'Yup.'

'Won't she try harder to be with you again?'

'It doesn't matter what she tries. She can't tear down this wall that defends my heart.'

'What do you mean?'

Instead of answering, Samuel changed the subject. 'Do you want to go for a swim?'

She nodded her head.

'I'll see you in the pool,' said Samuel.

I'd suppose swimming is more exciting than talking about ex-girlfriends, Kate thought, fetching her red swimmers with the white flowers on the side from her drawer. *These will do.*

Samuel surfaced from his dive into the warm water. He flicked his hair back. He rested his arms on the hard edge of the pool as he watched the rays of sunshine shimmer along the water like tiny colourful gemstones.

'Beautiful, isn't it?' asked a voice from behind.

Samuel jumped, making a splash. 'Don't do that!'

'Do what?' Kate asked.

'You nearly gave me a heart attack.'

'Don't blame me. You had your head in the clouds.'

Samuel rolled his eyes and turned his attention back towards the ocean.

'I know you don't want to share anything personal but...what was your ex-girlfriend like?' Kate wanted to know.

'She...she was kind of like you,' Samuel responded as he looked back at Kate.

'What does that mean?'

'She loved doing art. She was especially fond of all the zodiac signs.'

Art? Zodiac signs? Sounds like me in every way.

Then Kate saw that Samuel was crying again. 'You can stop if it hurts too much.'

'That's why I don't want to talk about her.'

'I'm sorry, uncle.'

The phone rang inside the house.

'I'll be back in a second.'

Poor man, Kate thought as Samuel climbed out of the pool and wrapped his towel around his waist before walking inside the house.

Kate wondered why Samuel's ex-girlfriend would break his gentle heart when he was every woman's dream guy. He was fit, had a high-paying job, an expensive car and a flashy house. Any woman would be delighted to live the lavish lifestyle with him.

Now I know why he isn't in a rush to have a relationship, Kate thought. *Whatever his ex-girlfriend did to him must've blown the flame out of his heart.*

A few minutes later, Samuel came back outside. He threw his towel onto the chair and then jumped back into the water.

'Who rang you this time?' Kate asked.

'Just Alex,' Samuel answered.

'What did she have to say?'

'She wanted to know if I'm still going ahead with the presentation tomorrow.'

'Oh...the presentation.' Kate immediately thought of Mary and her gang of sharks.

'Kate? Are you alright?' Samuel asked Kate.

'I...I...I'm not sure if I'll survive tomorrow with Mary,' Kate cried. 'She'll keep saying mean things about me!'

Samuel swam over and gently wrapped his arms around Kate. 'It's alright,' he whispered, 'I will not let Mary hurt you again.'

Chapter 6

WHY DID IT HAVE TO BE FRIDAY? WHY COULDN'T IT BE THE WEEKEND?
Kate grumbled at herself in the mirror while tying her hair up.

Kate was dressed in her white shirt that had butterflies flapping their blue wings in every direction. Her plain black skirt had pockets on each side of her hips. She even wore the hummingbird necklace that Samuel got for her.

She pocketed her phone and walked down the stairs, staring at the floor.

'Good morning,' said Samuel sitting at the dinner table eating his bowl of cornflakes.

Kate grabbed the cornflakes, the milk, and a bowl and placed them on the kitchen bench.

'Kate?' said Samuel as he watched Kate make her breakfast.

Kate still didn't speak as she took a spoon from the drawer. She didn't even look at Samuel as she sat down beside him.

'Is something wrong?' Samuel asked Kate.

Kate ate her cornflakes.

After several minutes of no response, Samuel placed his hand on Kate's shoulder.

Kate dropped her spoon into her bowl.

'What's wrong?'

'I'm scared of what Mary will say.'

'If anyone should be scared, it should be Mary.'

'What do you mean by that?'

'You'll see.'

Kate let out a low sigh, picked up her spoon and continued to eat her breakfast.

Once they were full, Kate collected her things from her room and then rejoined Samuel in the kitchen. He had set their lunchboxes and water bottles on the bench.

'Got everything?'

'I think so,' Kate replied in a low tone.

'Look, I know you're scared but just remember that karma will bite Mary in the butt.'

'I hope so.'

At the museum, Kate held the pile of museum bills and followed the history professor into the accounts department. The many workers greeted the pair, except for Jake. Jake was so busy typing his fingers away on the keyboard that he didn't notice the two of them arrive.

'Jake,' said Samuel.

Jake didn't flinch as he continued to type away.

'Jake,' Samuel said with a louder tone.

Jake turned his head at last. 'Oh, hi boss.'

Samuel took the bills from Kate and dropped them onto Jake's keyboard. 'Have fun paying the bills,' he said.

'Thanks, boss.'

With that, Samuel and Kate walked back to Samuel's office. Kate sat down at her table and pulled out her diary and pencil case.

'I'm going now,' said Samuel standing by the door.

'Okay,' Kate replied.

'Are you going to be alright sitting here while I'm gone?'

'Yes, uncle. I'll be sketching pictures in my diary.'

'Okay,' he said, 'I'll see you soon.'

With that, Samuel closed the door behind him.

Finally. Peace and quiet, Kate thought as she opened her diary.

Kate played her music on her phone out loud and then began to sketch her zodiac animal. The gentle vocalist echoed in her ears, blocking out the surrounding sounds. She didn't care if the lyrics were sung in a different language. The foreign vocals mixed with the instruments were the reason why she loved her artist. Each song expressed a human emotion.

She imagined her zodiac bull running through the forest, smashing everything in its path with its powerful horns. Every living thing either flew away or ran away in terror. None of them dared to face the rampaging beast.

Such a majestic and powerful beast, Kate thought, *I'm glad that I was born in May.*

After a while, Kate paused her music and looked at the rough outline of her zodiac animal in its charging stance. She wondered what Samuel would think of it.

'Well, well,' said a female voice.

Kate turned. Mary and a couple of her female friends were standing in Samuel's office. She jumped out of her chair, 'Mary?! W-what are you doing here in my uncle's office?'

'Such a big office for one man,' said Mary as she looked around the office.

'He is the boss after all,' said one of Mary's friends.

'Right! And all bosses have a slave to clean their shoes,' she Mary, looking straight at Kate.

'I-I'm not a slave!' Kate shouted.

Mary walked over to Kate's table and grabbed her diary.

'Hey! Give that back!'

Mary took one look at Kate's drawing and burst out laughing. 'What is this supposed to be?' she said. 'Your poor life?'

Kate tried to snatch the book out of Mary's hand but was pushed back instead.

Mary continued to laugh as she showed her friends the picture. The other girls join in Mary's mockery.

'Give me back my diary!' Kate demanded.

Mary gave Kate an evil smirk. 'You want your diary back?' she said. 'Sure!'

Kate gasped in horror as Mary ripped her picture from her book. She tried to grab her drawing from the floor, but Mary stomped on it.

'Stop it!' Kate ordered as tears poured down her face.

Mary, yet again, ignored Kate as she tore out her ideas and finished sketches. Once there was not a single page left, she dropped the book onto the floor.

No! Kate cried as she dropped onto her hands and knees.

'That's more like it,' said Mary, 'a crying little peasant.'

Kate gritted her teeth. She looked up at Mary with rage burning inside her eyes and her body. 'You will pay for that!'

The three girls laughed at Kate's threat.

'Oh? And what are you going to do about it, peasant?' said Mary. 'My daddy can easily fire your parents with just one phone call.'

Kate's rage grew inside her. She was nearly at the point of unleashing her inner Taurus fury at Mary and her friends.

'Nothing,' said Mary. 'Just as I thought.'

Mary walked over to Samuel's bookshelf. She scanned through the books until she found a book about Pompeii and Herculaneum. She pulled it out and looked at the cover for a moment. She then turned her attention back toward Kate.

'You should've seen Professor Wood's presentation. He's such a brilliant man,' said Mary. 'Oh wait! Ugly peasants like you aren't allowed to see him.'

'If you don't put that book back on the shelf, I will call security!' Kate warned Mary.

Mary rolled her eyes and then let the book fall out of her hands and onto the floor. She then grabbed another book and began to tear the pages out of it. Her friends joined in on the action.

You've done it now, Kate thought as she got up to her feet.

She grabbed her phone from the table and rang Shawn. After explaining the situation to him, she went into her camera app and took take several pictures while Mary and her friends were busy laughing and destroying Samuel's books.

'Let's see how you like it when you anger a history professor,' said Kate through her tears as she texted Samuel.

After a while of demolishing Samuel's books, Mary walked up to Kate with her arms crossed. 'You are going to be in so much trouble when I tell Professor Wood that you destroyed his books.'

Shawn and two other security guards ran into the office.

'Are you alright, Miss Summer?' Shawn asked Kate.

'Oh! Thank goodness you showed up,' Mary said innocently. 'This poor-looking girl broke into Professor Wood's office and destroyed all his books. I tried to stop her, but she didn't listen to me.'

Shawn and the security guards looked at the pile of demolished books. They saw the many pages ripped and torn all over the floor.

'Professor Wood is going to be pissed off when he sees this,' said Shawn.

'I know, that's why this girl needs to pay for the damage she caused,' said Mary.

'She needs to be kicked out of the museum,' suggested one of Mary's friends.

'What's going on?' demanded a voice.

Shawn and the guards got out of the way as Samuel walked into his office.

'What's going on?' Samuel repeated his question to Kate.

Kate quickly pointed at the pile of books that Mary and her friends destroyed.

As soon as Samuel saw the mess, his jaw dropped. His eyes widened in shock.

'My books!' he shouted. 'What happened to my books?!'

'Well, Professor,' said Mary as she walked up to the professor. 'This stranger got into your office and destroyed your precious history books. I tried to warn her, but she didn't listen to me.'

'Uncle, you know that I would never destroy your books,' said Kate.

'Professor Wood is not your uncle,' Mary argued, 'you don't even look remotely related to him.'

'Enough!' Samuel roared.

The entire room fell silent.

Samuel sighed. 'I'm indeed single but that doesn't mean I'm alone in this world.' He looked at Kate. 'I'm afraid you need to leave the museum immediately.'

Mary looked at Kate with an evil smirk on her face. 'Goodbye, peasant girl,' she said.

'Not Kate; I was talking to you.'

Mary's smirk was quickly wiped off her face. 'What?!' she said as Shawn took her by the arm.

The two other security guards grabbed Mary's friends.

'Why should I leave? I didn't do anything wrong,' said Mary as she struggled to free her arm from Shawn's grip.

'No one threatens my niece and gets away with it,' Samuel answered as he wrapped his arm around Kate.

With that, the three security guards took Mary and her friends out of Samuel's office.

Samuel waited until he no longer heard Mary's voice before hugging Kate. 'Are you alright?'

'No,' Kate sobbed. 'Mary destroyed my diary.'

Samuel looked down and saw the torn pages from Kate's diary. Nothing was left of the diary but the cover and the back.

That leech has caused enough damage, Samuel grumbled, *it's time for her to learn to stop hurting people.*

'Do you have any photos of Mary?' he asked Kate gently.

Kate nodded her head.

'Can you send them to me?'

Kate freed herself from Samuel's arms and then wiped her tears with her hand. She then grabbed her phone and sent the photos to Samuel.

Kate picked up the torn picture of her zodiac animal. Her teardrops splashed onto the paper. She couldn't believe that her powerful and stubborn animal had been killed by Mary's greed and jealousy. She crumpled the picture into a ball then threw the picture into the bin underneath Samuel's desk.

'Hey, if you want, we can visit an art shop on Monday and see if they have any diaries,' said Samuel.

'I don't just want any diary,' said Kate. 'I want the same one I had.'

Samuel nodded.

Kate wiped her tears while Samuel rang his cleaners to clean up the mess. Then Samuel rang Jake and requested him to order new history books. He did not mention anything about Mary or the damage she and her friends had done to his office. When Jake began to question him, he immediately hung up.

'Do you want to use my notepad?' Samuel asked Kate.

'It has lines on it,' Kate replied. 'I don't like my drawings with lines in them.'

'Draw on the back.'

'Fine.'

Samuel handed his notepad to Kate. She took it back to her table and tried her best to forget about Mary destroying her diary. She focused on re-sketching her zodiac animal. She tried to re-imagine the powerful beast but couldn't. Her memory kept repeating Mary destroying her art projects. Some of her pictures had taken her weeks or months. She remembers the way Samuel smiled whenever she finished a picture. But now, there was nothing left of her heart.

Kate took out her phone and played her music out loud instead of getting her headphones from her bag.

Samuel wanted to ask Kate to turn down the music but didn't. He stayed quiet and endured the pain of Kate's favourite artist.

Sometime later, a group of cleaners walked into Samuel's office. Their eyes were quickly drawn to the destroyed books.

'What happened here, professor?' asked one of the cleaners.

'A few students came in and destroyed my books,' Samuel answered.

'Oh my gosh! What are you going to do with them?' asked another cleaner.

'Don't worry about that. I've got that sorted out.'

Two of the cleaners started to pick up the torn and ripped pages while the other two picked up the empty covers.

Samuel rose to pick up the pieces of Kate's destroyed diary. He then walked back to his desk and threw the pile into his bin. Then he sat at his desk, opened the email and began to write.

'You and your friends better not show your face in front of Kate again,' Samuel said softly.

After the long paragraph, Samuel pressed the send button. All he could do now was to wait for the result.

The cleaners finished cleaning then quietly left Samuel's office. By that time, Samuel's stomach growled like a hungry lion.

'Man, I'm starving,' said Samuel then turned to Kate. 'Hey, are you hungry?'

Kate didn't put down her pencil.

'Kate?'

Samuel went over to Kate. He placed his hand onto her shoulder, but she didn't take her eyes off her picture.

'Honey Dragon?'

Kate slowly placed her pencil down and then paused her music. She then looked up at Samuel with sad eyes.

'Are you hungry?' Samuel asked.

'No,' she replied. 'After what Mary did to me, I don't feel hungry.'

'I know Mary destroyed your ideas and sketches, but why don't you start over?'

Kate yanked Samuel by his tie until her flaming hot eyes stared into his eyes. 'Start over?!' she shouted. 'Some of my pictures took me forever to complete! You always smile at my pictures. My pictures make you smile! Now that my work is gone, I won't ever see you smile again!'

'That's not the reason why I smile,' said Samuel as he freed his tie from Kate.

'What?'

'I do love your artwork but that's what makes you happy, not me.'

'If my artwork doesn't make you smile, what does?'

'Having my artistic niece in my life is what makes me smile.'

The last of Kate's remaining tears rolled down her cheeks as a weak smile formed across her face. She immediately forgot about Mary destroying her diary.

'Now, who's hungry?' Samuel asked.

'Are we going to eat in the staff room?' Kate asked Samuel as she grabbed her lunchbox from her bag.

Instead of answering Kate, Samuel pulled out his lunch container and his fork from his bag. He then pushed his chair over to Kate's table and sat down.

'What are you doing?' Kate asked Samuel.

'I want to have lunch with you,' Samuel replied. 'Plus, I want to know about all the zodiac signs.'

'Why?'

'I'm curious.'

Kate immediately knew that Samuel would not listen to a word because she knew that he didn't believe in astrology. 'You know that I'm only going to explain this once,' she said.

'I'm all ears,' said Samuel as he ate his lunch.

Kate stated all the zodiac signs in order. Starting with Aries, the ram animal sign, to the last sign, Pisces, the fish. She then explained their special talents and spiritual powers.

Geez, Samuel thought, pretending to listen to Kate, *astrology can really put someone to sleep.*

After lunch and the long story, Samuel's exhausted brain felt like a balloon slowly deflating.

'So, did you learn something from me?' Kate asked with a smile.

'You lost me after the Aries sign,' Samuel answered.

'Uncle!'

Samuel let out a soft chuckle. 'I'm just kidding,' he said as he patted Kate's back. 'I'm just happy that you're smiling again.'

'You're right. Except...'

'Except what?'

'Why did you ask for those photos?'

Samuel continued to pat Kate's back. 'You'll find out on Tuesday.'

Chapter 7

KATE DRAGGED HER HALF-ASLEEP BODY DOWN THE STAIRS. HER eyes were instantly drawn to Samuel, who was in the kitchen dressed in a plain grey shirt and plain track pants. His blue gym bag sat on the edge of the kitchen bench ready to go.

'Morning, uncle,' said Kate as she grabbed the box of cornflakes from the cupboard.

'Hey,' Samuel replied as he placed the sliced fruit into the blender.

Kate walked over to where Samuel was standing and grabbed a bowl and a spoon from the drawer. She then got a bottle of milk from the fridge.

'Milk is already out if you need it,' said Samuel.

'Why bother when you're going to drink the rest anyway?' Kate pointed out as she poured the cereal into her bowl.

Samuel paused. 'I hate it when you're right.'

'I'm always right,' she said as she poured the milk into her bowl and then sat down at the dinner table.

'Sometimes.'

Samuel added the milk to the blender and then placed the lid on top. He pressed the button on the machine and watched as the fruit swirled around like a tornado. Slowly breaking up into pieces until it finally turned into a red liquid.

He poured the smoothie into a glass then sat down next to Kate.

'Hey uncle, can I ask you something about your ex-girlfriend?' said Kate.

'No,' Samuel answered then took a sip from his cup.

'Please! I really want to know.'

'It better not be anything about how we met or stuff like that.'

'No.'

He sighed. 'What do you want to know?'

'Was your ex-girlfriend that beautiful that you gave up dating other women?'

Samuel placed his cup down. 'Look, it doesn't matter if she was beautiful or not. The main reason I'm still single is because of her cheating on me with–'

'With whom?'

'I'm going,' said Samuel as he hurried over to the sink.

He poured the remaining, mostly undrunk smoothie down the drain. He was so upset that he didn't even rinse the cup.

Kate could see how hurt Samuel was and was desperately curious to know what this mysterious woman had done to hurt him so deeply.

'Did she cheat with someone you knew?' Kate asked, trying to sound sympathetic.

'Goodbye!' Samuel shouted as he grabbed his keys, phone and bag then went into the garage and slammed the door behind him.

His angry determination not to answer her only made Kate more curious about his secrets.

Kate cleared away her breakfast dishes, then finished dressing and tying her hair back before picking up her phone and calling her friend Sebastian.

When Sebastian finally answered, Kate was greeted by one of Sebastian's favourite wrestler's theme songs playing loudly in the background.

'Sebastian!' Kate shouted.

'Sorry!' said Sebastian then turned off his music. 'You know that I love the Viper.'

Kate, who loved gentle music, disliked Sebastian's taste in music. He preferred wrestling theme songs as well as old rock songs.

'Yes,' she said as she rolled her eyes. 'I know.'

'Do you want to know my other favourite wrestlers?'

'No thanks. I was just calling to see if you liked the presentation from yesterday.'

'Why weren't you at school for an entire week?' Sebastian asked, changing the subject.

Kate let out a sigh and then explained to Sebastian that Mary's hurtful comments were like an arrow that had been shot deep into her gentle heart and that it couldn't be pulled out. Samuel was the only person who managed to pull out the arrow and allow her heart to heal by resting at home instead of attending school.

'I wished that I'd stayed home for a week,' said Sebastian, 'but no! I had to be picked on by Mary.'

'I'm sorry,' Kate replied.

'I wish that Mary would never show her face again.'

'Don't worry. Uncle Samuel said to wait until Tuesday.'

Sebastian paused for a brief second. 'What do you mean by that?'

'I don't know. He said those words, not me.'

Half an hour later, Kate said goodbye to Sebastian, hung up and crossed the bridge into Samuel's office.

Kate wondered if Samuel still had the letter from his ex-girlfriend. Perhaps she could find a clue in it without having to upset Samuel again by asking. She looked underneath Samuel's desk.

She pulled a paper ball out of the bin. She unfolded the crumpled paper but didn't read the letter. Instead, her eyes were drawn to the bottom of the letter where she saw the name *Summer* written in a cursive font.

'Why are you trying to get back together with my uncle when you already broke his heart, Summer?' Kate wondered aloud.

Kate knew that Samuel would never say another word about Summer. Even if Kate tried to ask him, she'd only make him upset or angry.

I wish that I knew more about your ex-girlfriend, she thought as she crushed the letter back into a ball and then threw it into the bin and went to her studio.

Kate passed the time by painting a pink rose with a rainbow-coloured butterfly sitting on the rose's leaf.

Nearly four hours later, Kate heard the front door slamming. She placed her paintbrush down on the table and then walked out of her studio and downstairs. She went to greet him only to be hit by a wave of smelly body odour that circled his body like a cloud.

'Gross!' said Kate as she blocked her nose.

'What?' said Samuel as he dumped his bag onto the kitchen bench.

'Don't you ever wear deodorant after working out?'

'Only after taking a shower.'

'Why don't you use the gym's showers?'

Samuel looked at Kate with his eyebrow raised.

'Oh…right, women.'

Samuel took his shoes and socks off and then walked into the backyard with Kate following from behind.

Kate sat down on a pool chair and watched Samuel as he took his shirt off and threw it onto the ground. He then walked to the edge of the pool.

'Should you–'

Kate's sentence was cut off by the sound of Samuel as he splashed into the pool.

'Take your pants off before getting into the pool? Never mind,' she sighed.

Samuel came up to the surface and flicked his hair out of his face.

'That's better,' he said. 'At least now that I don't smell like sweat.'

'Yeah, you'll smell like chlorine instead,' Kate replied.

Samuel ignored Kate's last sentence and then went back underwater.

Kate got off her chair, walked over to the edge of the pool, sat down on the cold ground and put her feet into the pool.

Once again, Samuel flicked his hair back when he came to the surface. After that, he got out of the pool, grabbed a towel, wrapped it around his waist, and then sat down beside Kate.

'I bet you're happy tomorrow,' said Kate.

'What's happening tomorrow?' Samuel wanted to know.

'You're going with Jake to the bar, remember?'

'Oh, right! I forgot about that.'

'You'll be happy to get away from me tomorrow.'

'Not really.'

'And why not?'

'I'm just worried that I'm leaving you alone with Sebastian and that something bad will happen while I'm gone.'

'We're fifteen years old, uncle. We can take care of ourselves.'

'I know, but–'

'No, buts. I want to see you fully relaxed when you get home tomorrow.'

Samuel turned his attention away from Kate.

'When was the last time you went to a bar?'

'When I was eighteen years old,' he said, looking back at Kate.

'Wow! You really do need to relax for a bit.'

'That's what I'm worried about.'

'Uncle.'

'I'm not sure if I'll survive tomorrow.'

'Uncle!'

Samuel instantly went quiet.

'Everything will be alright tomorrow. If anything does happen, me or Sebastian will ring you.'

Samuel went to open his mouth but was stopped by Kate.

'Promise me that you'll relax tomorrow,' she said.

'I'll try,' Samuel sighed.

'You better or else I'm going to send you out again.'

Samuel let out a chuckle. 'If I go out again, I'll come back as a drunken person.'

'I ain't helping you if you come home drunk.'

Samuel let out another chuckle. 'No. I'll just try and relax tomorrow.'

'You better hope so,' she said as she rested her head against Samuel's arm.

Samuel smiled at Kate and then looked out onto the ocean.

Oh, boy, he thought, nervously.

Chapter 8

Samuel wasn't sure if he'd made the right choice. He wasn't sure if it was alright to leave Kate alone with Sebastian for a few hours while he and Jake went to their favourite sports bar.

'Do you think they'll be alright by themselves?' Samuel asked his friend, looking out the window of Jake's car.

'Relax, man!' said Jake, 'they'll be fine.'

'Are you sure? They're still young.'

'They're fifteen years old. They can look after themselves for a few hours.'

Samuel let out a soft sigh as he turned his attention back towards the window.

I hope so, he thought.

Meanwhile, Kate was in her art studio painting her animal nickname. Sebastian was curiously looking at her paintings.

'Your paintings,' said Sebastian.

'What about them?' said Kate, not taking her brush off the canvas.

'They're beautiful.'

'You're just saying that because we're friends.'

'No. I mean, how do you come up with these brilliant designs?'

'Well, I dream a lot.'

Sebastian casually walked past Kate at her easel to examine a vase on her desk. Kate had hand-made the terracotta-coloured ceramic vase full of fake-looking ceramic pink roses a few years ago in art class. She'd also created smaller ceramic pencil holders for her art supplies, each decorated with a different realistic-looking flower.

Sebastian slowly looked up at Kate's bookshelf that stood above her desk. Her bookshelf was filled with old art diaries that she kept over the years. She even had textbooks that Samuel bought for her to read and learn.

He noticed something was missing. 'Hey Kate,' said Sebastian.

'Yes?' Kate replied.

'Where's your art diary?'

Kate placed her paints down and turned. 'What did you say?'

Sebastian pointed at the empty spot on the bookshelf. 'Didn't you have a diary with some symbol on it?'

Kate looked away from Sebastian as she rubbed the sides of her arms. 'Someone destroyed it,' she said.

'Who destroyed your diary?'

'Who's the one person that hates the two of us?'

'Mary?'

Kate nodded her head. 'Yes.'

'How could Mary destroy your diary when you weren't at school?'

Kate told Sebastian about what had happened in Samuel's office on the day of the presentation.

'They destroyed every single book of Samuel's?' said Sebastian.

Kate nodded her head.

'Oh my gosh!'

'Yeah. Samuel was not happy when he saw the books.'

'Is your uncle going to make the girls pay for the books?'

Kate shook her head. 'No.'

'Is he going to talk to the principal?'

Kate shook her head again.

'What is he going to do then?'

'All he said is to wait until Tuesday.'

'If I was Samuel, I would make Mary and her friends pay for every single book,' Sebastian said as he crossed his arms.

'Me too.'

A few hours later, the friends heard chatter from downstairs. They went downstairs to find Jake and Samuel happily chattering and laughing.

'Welcome home,' said Sebastian.

'Hey, son,' said Jake.

'I'm guessing by your reactions that you two survived at the bar,' said Kate.

'Oh! It was brilliant. Except we kept getting rudely interrupted by women wanting to hang out with Samuel.'

'Of course,' Sebastian replied.

'Other than that, we survived.'

'I'm glad you talked me into going with you to our favourite bar,' Samuel said to Jake.

'Anytime, boss.'

'I wish we could do this every Sunday but I'm a busy guy.'

'I understand. You have a museum to run, and you have a family to raise.' Jake then turned his attention to Sebastian. 'Well, we better get going. We have a video game shop to get to.'

'Really?' said Sebastian.

'Yes, sir.'

'Thanks, dad!'

'Grab your phone, say your goodbye to Kate and then we'll go.'

Sebastian rushed over to the kitchen and grabbed his phone from the dinner table. He then went back to Kate and said goodbye to her before running out the front door.

'Well,' Jake said to Samuel. 'I'll see you at work on Tuesday.'

'I'll see you Tuesday then,' Samuel replied.

'Bye, Kate.'

'Bye, Jake,' Kate said.

With that, Jake walked out the front door and then closed it behind him.

'I think you should be called a woman magnet instead of muscle god,' said Kate as she walked up to Samuel.

'No, thanks,' Samuel replied. 'They both sound worse.'

'Think about it. Women can't resist seeing a handsome, famous history professor like you.'

'They only love me because I'm famous. If I didn't own a museum or was a history professor, everyone would see me as an everyday person.'

'I guess that's true.'

Samuel grabbed his wallet from his pocket and then walked over to the kitchen and placed it on the bench.

'So, tell me,' said Kate as she went over to Samuel. 'Are you finally relaxed?'

'Can I leave you here and go out again?' said Samuel.

'Uncle!'

'Just kidding,' he laughed.

Kate shook her head with annoyance.

'I'm just happy that I was able to relax for a few hours.'

'See, I told you. There was no reason for you to be worried about leaving me and Sebastian alone.'

'I know, but you know what I'm like.'

'A protective uncle that is a woman magnet.'

Samuel shook his head and then walked over to the fridge and pulled out a water bottle.

'It's true though,' said Kate.

'I sometimes wonder why I ended up with someone else's child,' Samuel replied in Japanese as he took a sip of water.

'What did you say, uncle? I didn't understand you.'

'Nothing,' he said in English. 'I was just thinking about work.'

'Do I have to call Jake and ask him to take you out again?'

'No thanks. Besides, we have a public holiday tomorrow, remember?'

'So what?'

'So, we can get your diary, remember?'

'Oh, right! I forgot.'

Samuel then took another sip and then put the bottle back into the fridge.

'I'll try and find the address in the morning before we go, okay?'

'Yes, uncle.'

With that, Samuel left the kitchen and went upstairs to his bedroom, leaving Kate alone in the kitchen.

I just hope they have my diary, Kate thought.

Chapter 9

THE NEXT MORNING, KATE WAS SITTING NEXT TO SAMUEL AT THE dinner table watching him scrolling through every art shop throughout Night Valley.

'Don't you remember where you got my diary?' Kate asked Samuel.

'No,' Samuel replied, 'I don't even remember where the shop was.'

'It's down the coast, remember? Moon Art shop was the name.'

'Moon Art shop! Now I remember.'

Kate rolled her eyes as Samuel looked up the directions. 'Honestly, uncle,' she said, 'I think you're getting to that age where you start forgetting things.'

'Hey!' Samuel protested, 'I'm not that old yet. And I'll keep reading and learning about the world's past until the day I retire,' he added. 'By then, I'll have more time to read my history books.'

'You and your books,' Kate grumbled.

After a minute or two, Samuel found the shop's address. 'Bingo!' he said. 'Let's go.'

Once they were both in the car, Samuel typed the address into his GPS.

'While we're down the coast, I want to grab a smoothie,' said Samuel.

'Can I have a chocolate milkshake?' said Kate.

'Of course.'

Samuel and Kate arrived at several shops that looked like they were movie sets.

'Here we are,' said Samuel as he parked his car in front of Moon Art shop.

Kate was out of the car even before Samuel could turn off the engine. She ran inside the art shop, letting the glass door bang shut behind her.

'Good morning,' greeted the female staff member standing behind the counter.

Kate greeted the woman back and then walked down the aisle where they had endless rows of sketch pads, diaries and scrapbooks. On the other side of the aisle, they had stacks of coloured paper. Some had different patterns on them. Hanging next to the papers were packets of stickers on hooks.

Kate slowly walked down the aisle until she found a shelf that had all the zodiac signs in order. She carefully pulled out her Taurus bull that stood next to the Aries and gazed at the cover that was as dark as the night. In the middle of the cover was her sign as a golden-coloured constellation. Even the name was printed in gold. At the base of the spine, the Taurus symbol was also printed in gold.

This book doesn't look like my old one, Kate thought then let out a soft sigh. *I guess it wouldn't hurt to start over.*

'Do you need a hand with anything?' asked a female voice.

'No thanks,' Kate answered then looked up at the woman.

Both Kate and the woman gasped in shock.

The woman had the same majestic hazel eyes, fair skin and long brown hair as Kate but tied up with a red hair tie. It was like she was looking at herself but in ten years.

'By the mighty Taurus,' said the woman, 'is it really you, Kate?'

'H-how do you know my name?'

Before the woman could answer, Samuel walked up beside Kate. 'Did you find the book you were looking for?'

'I think so,' Kate answered.

'Samuel,' said the woman. She went to hug the man only to be pushed back.

'Don't you dare touch me, Summer!' Samuel shouted.

Samuel took Kate's hand and dragged her to the counter. He paid for the book and then stormed out of the shop.

The two of them got into the car and drove away in complete silence. Neither of them looked at each other nor did they talk to each other for a solid twenty minutes until they arrived at a small café that stood across from the friendly, gentle ocean.

Inside, the café was filled with soft music in the background that no one paid attention to. Customers happily chattered among themselves as they filled their stomachs with freshly made food and drinks that tasted like they were made by the gods.

Samuel walked up to the counter and ordered their drinks while Kate sat at a table next to the giant glass window.

Through the window, Kate watched the gentle waves flow up and down the sand while the seagulls floated along the surface of the water like paper boats. The peaceful scene reminded her of a painting that she had done for art class a few years ago.

Samuel arrived at the table. 'Here you go,' he said as he placed the drinks down and then sat next to Kate.

'Thanks, uncle,' said Kate as she grabbed her milkshake and took a small sip through the straw. 'What did you get?'

'A banana smoothie.'

How original, Kate thought then changed the subject. 'About that woman from the art shop.'

'No.'

'You didn't let me finish what I was about to say.'

'I don't care what you were going to say! I do not want to hear anything else about that woman.'

Kate faced the window and quietly drank her milkshake. *All I wanted to know was how she knew my name. Was she your ex-girlfriend? Is she somehow related to me?*

'I want a vanilla milkshake!' demanded a voice.

Kate, Samuel, and the entire room turned towards the counter.

'Oh boy!' said Samuel, noticing Mary dressed in expensive clothes from head to toe acting like a five-year-old throwing a tantrum in the shopping centre.

A man who had the same-coloured eyes as Mary, dressed in an expensive-looking grey suit with his large stomach hanging out, stood a metre away from the girl with his phone glued to his gigantic ear. A small patch on the back of his head was as smooth as glass while the rest of his head was filled with silver hair.

'Give me a vanilla milkshake! Now!' Mary demanded the staff at the top of her lungs.

'Mary is acting like a three-year-old over a milkshake,' said Kate with her eyebrow raised in annoyance. 'Seriously, how low can that spoiled girl go?'

'Low enough to get people to obey her commands,' Samuel replied.

Kate slowly shook her head. 'I'm glad you didn't raise me to be like Mary,' she said, 'otherwise I would've been a shark instead of a hummingbird.'

'That's why it's best to live a normal, simple life and not brag about the amount of money you have in the bank.'

'Yeah,' she said then took another sip of her drink.

After several minutes of watching Mary throwing a fit, two security guards came up to her and forcefully dragged her out of the café by her arms. The older man followed them, while ordering them to release the girl.

Samuel and Kate had finished their drinks and made their way to the car only to find Mary and the older man talking beside a black expensive-looking car.

'They're still here,' Kate whispered.

'Just get in the car and pay no attention to them,' Samuel replied.

Kate lowered her head as she got into the car. Samuel was about to get beside her when he was stopped by the older man.

Oh no, Kate thought as the man and Mary approached Samuel.

'You!' the man roared at Samuel.

'Oh, hi Mr Johnson,' Samuel said calmly.

'How dare you publicly humiliate my daughter?!'

'What do you mean?'

'You kicked her out of the museum when all she was doing was enjoying the trip!'

'She broke a rule.'

'Oh, like what? Destroying some boring ancient vase.'

'No, she invaded my office and destroyed my books.'

'So what? They are just a bunch of pages with writing and pictures on them.'

'Excuse me?!'

Oh no, Kate thought.

'That goes the same for your museum. It's filled with nothing but a bunch of boring items,' said Mr Johnson. 'Eventually, you'll have no choice but to sell your museum.'

Samuel crossed his arms. 'I will never sell my museum of wonder to an oversize bastard like you.'

Ouch!

'Well,' said Mr Johnson as he fixed his suit. 'Don't come begging to me once your business fails.'

Samuel ignored Mr Johnson as he and Mary got into the expensive car and drove off. He let out a soft sigh and then got into his car.

'Are you alright, uncle?' Kate asked Samuel.

'I'm fine,' Samuel answered. 'In fact, I'm quite surprised with Mr Johnson.'

'How are you surprised?'

'He thinks that my museum would fail and that I would sell it to him.'

'How can your museum fail when you're famous?'

'He doesn't think because he's a dodo.'

Kate burst out in laughter. 'You're not wrong there, uncle.'

'He might be rich now, but sooner or later his thirst for money will be his downfall.'

'I hope it is.'

With that, they went to the Broadwater and walked side by side along the cement path beside each other. Samuel's eyes gazed upon the smiling river. Small sailing boats skimmed along the surface of the water like they were people skating on land. Seagulls and other birds flew past the two like rockets and over the buildings that stood across from the river.

'The water looks stunning,' said Samuel. 'What do you think?'

The only response Samuel got was the sound of the wind as it blew through his hair. He stopped in the middle of the path and then turned to find Kate standing next to a large tree, looking up into the branches.

'Kate?'

'Aren't they beautiful?' said Kate.

'I don't see anything.'

Kate walked closer to the tree and then pointed up at the branches. Samuel slowly walked closer to Kate. He searched and scanned through every leaf and every branch until he found a pair of lorikeets happily sitting on a branch chirping loudly high up in the tree.

'I don't know how you managed to spot those birds,' said Samuel.

'I've got the vision of a hummingbird remember,' Kate replied. 'Nothing gets past my eyes.'

More like the vision of an eagle, Samuel thought as he watched Kate walk towards the bench that looked out onto the river and sat down. He joined her.

She was silent for a long time.

'What's on your mind?' Samuel asked.

'The woman from the shop,' said Kate. She sensed Samuel becoming tense again and sighed. 'I want to know more.'

'Forget her.'

'I can't. She knew my name. I think she was your ex.' Kate knew there had to be more to the mystery, but it was a good place to start.

'If I tell you, will you stop asking about her?'

Kate nodded.

'I met the love of my life in this exact spot.'

'Here? On this bench?'

'I was on holidays at the time.'

Kate covered her mouth with her hand as she snickered.

'What's so funny?'

'I can just imagine you spending your holidays with your phone glued to your ear,' said Kate.

'No! I was actually relaxing, believe it or not.'

'Sure.'

Samuel went back to telling his story. 'I was doing my usual morning jog when I saw this beautiful woman painting on her canvas.' Samuel then let out a flirtatious sigh. 'She was like an angel.'

'Keep going, Romeo.'

'I took a break from jogging and sat down next to her. I couldn't take my eyes off her painting the Broadwater. It was so realistic that it could easily be mistaken for a photograph. At first, I said nothing, but once I'd built up my courage, I couldn't stop talking with her about art.'

'I didn't know you had a thing for art,' said Kate.

'I did when I was younger.'

'And now?'

Samuel slowly raised his eyebrow. Kate slid her thumb and index finger across her mouth like she was zipping a zipper.

'After a while of talking about art, the woman gave me her phone number and her name,' Samuel continued. 'After that, we went on dates.'

'Until she broke your heart.'

'Yeah...' he mumbled as he lowered his head.

'I'm sorry you went through that,' she replied as she rested her head on Samuel's shoulder.

'Well,' Samuel responded as he looked back at Kate, 'I'd rather raise you than have a relationship.'

'Excuse me, professor,' said a voice.

Samuel turned his head and saw a skinny man wearing a plain green shirt and black pants that had small holes in them. His black running shoes were covered in a dry layer of mud. His head was covered in tiny hairs. A small silver piercing sat above and underneath the man's left eyebrow while a larger piercing ran out his right nostril. He had dirt under some of his fingernails.

'Can I help you, sir?' Samuel asked the man as he tried not to breathe in the foul cigarette smell that surrounded the man like a shield.

'I was watching you from a distance and was wondering if this kid was annoying you,' replied the man.

'Why would she be annoying me when we're both talking?'

Instead of answering the question, the man turned his attention to Kate. 'Are you lost, young lady? Where is your family?'

Kate was about to answer when Samuel interrupted.

'Listen here you! Just leave us alone and we won't have any problems, okay?' Samuel was trying to not raise his voice.

'Come on sir! This teenage brat obviously ran away from her family just to bother your busy day.'

'Excuse me?!'

Kate instantly lifted her head off Samuel's shoulder when she saw his face glowing brightly red. She knew that Samuel was about to explode like a volcano, and she rarely saw him turn from a fun, lovable uncle to her zodiac animal.

'What did you call my niece?!' Samuel roared as he quickly got up onto his feet.

The man tried to calm down Samuel but was quickly yanked by his shirt.

'Listen here, you bastard! No one calls my niece a brat.'

'I...I didn't know she was your niece,' quaked the man, 'I thought she was separated from her family.'

'Well, she isn't separated! She's the only family I've got, and I will not allow a punk like you to judge us without fully knowing us. Got it?!'

The man nodded his head endlessly until Samuel pushed him onto the hard ground.

'Get out of here before I call the police!' Samuel ordered.

The man quickly picked himself up and ran away from Samuel and Kate faster than a bullet.

'You'd think people would realise by now that I'm your niece,' said Kate.

'Unfortunately, no,' Samuel replied with a normal tone as he sat back down next to Kate. 'People will only see us as a joke just because we're born with different nationalities.'

'That's true but they forgot something very important.'

'And what's that?' he asked, looking at Kate.

'Family isn't about what we look like on the outside. Family is about love, warmth, and joy.'

A smile formed across Samuel's face, knowing that he had taught Kate well with important life lessons.

'Can we go home now? I want to go for a swim.'

'Of course, Honey Dragon.'

With that, Kate jumped to her feet and sprinted back to the car while Samuel casually made his way to his car.

Kate was happily watching the calm ocean from the edge of the pool until she was interrupted by Samuel coming out of the water beside her.

'How's the view?' Samuel asked Kate.

'It's great,' Kate answered, 'I thought of a few ideas for a painting.'

'I honestly don't know how you and every other artist on this planet come up with such...'

'Imaginative masterpieces?'

Samuel nodded his head. 'Yeah.'

'Well, all great masterpieces start with a simple idea.' Kate then pointed at the ocean. 'Take the ocean for example. I see more than just water. I see another world under the surface.'

'If you say so, Honey Dragon.'

Kate turned towards Samuel. 'You need to use a bit of imagination, uncle.'

'I wish I could, but I have work tomorrow and you have school.'

Oh no! Kate thought.

Chapter 10

WHY COULDN'T IT BE THE WEEKEND ALREADY? KATE THOUGHT, walking past the sports hall with her eyes lowered to the ground.

Kate didn't want to spend another day being bullied by Mary and her friends. She wanted to stay at home and annoy Samuel with her music. Or even paint a picture.

I hope Mary isn't at school today. Knowing my luck, she will be.

Kate made her way to her locker while paying no attention to the students that were laughing and pointing fingers at her from left and right. When she reached the canteen area, Kate kept her head down as she quietly passed a large table that was full of the popular male students. Mostly the handsome, tall, athletic type.

Don't look at me, Kate repeated over and over.

Unfortunately, one of the guys turned his head and spotted Kate walking to her locker with her head down.

'Hey guys, look who it is,' whispered the student.

'Ugh! Seriously?' whispered another student. 'What is she wearing?'

'I know right. She must've gotten those clothes from the garbage bin.'

Kate saw them laughing at her. She let out a sad sigh as opened her locker.

'Are you alright, Kate?' asked a familiar voice. Sebastian walked up to her with a worried look on his face.

'No,' Kate answered, 'I'm just sick and tired of people mocking me.'

'I know how exactly you feel,' Sebastian replied then opened to his own locker. 'People mock me for being weird.'

'That's mostly from Mary. But still, I just want to come to school and not have people bully me.'

'Knowing us, that day will never come.' He placed his school bag into his locker and then closed it.

'I just hope my uncle's plan works today,' Kate sighed as she locked her bag away too.

'If not?' Sebastian questioned Kate as the two of them made their way to Ancient History class.

'Then I give up.'

The two friends walked inside the classroom to find a woman sitting at the table, tapping away on her laptop with her red-coloured nails. Her long ginger hair was tied up in a braid that flowed down her spine. She wore a plain white blouse and a long red skirt that flowed near her ankles. Her blue eyes were covered by gigantic circular glasses that sat on the bridge of her nose. Tiny little emerald gemstones in the shape of a love heart dangled from the woman's ears.

'Morning, Mrs Ruby,' said Sebastian as he sat down next to Kate in the front row.

'Morning Kate, morning Sebastian,' said Mrs Ruby as she looked up from her laptop.

Mrs Ruby was Kate's and Sebastian's English teacher. She used to be a well-known author before she became a teacher. She would make her students write a short story on paper at the beginning of every lesson as she wanted her students to keep practising their handwriting instead of relying on technology to write for them. Some said was old-fashioned, but she always believed that it was best to keep the ability to write with a pen or pencil.

'Where's Mr Winter?' Sebastian asked Mrs Ruby.

'He's at a meeting this morning,' Mrs Ruby answered, 'so I'll be taking over for him until then.'

Mrs Ruby then turned her attention to Kate. 'How's your uncle going?'

'He's busy as usual,' Kate answered.

'Is he still looking for Miss Perfect?'

'We were talking about that last week, and he's decided to care for me rather than search for the perfect woman.'

'Fair enough. If he's happy raising you alone, then let him enjoy that lifestyle.'

'Say that to the single ladies,' Sebastian whispered to Kate as the school bell rang.

Students poured into the classroom and sat down. Once the sound of chattering died down, Mrs Ruby stood in front of the table. 'Good morning students,' she said with a smile on her face, 'unfortunately, Mr Winter is in a meeting this morning and cannot teach.'

'He could've gotten Professor Wood to teach us,' said a female student.

Mrs Ruby ignored the student. 'Mr Winter has sent you all an email with the list of work you need to do.'

'I hope it's not about Pompeii and Herculaneum again,' Sebastian grumbled as everyone logged into their computers.

'What were you hoping for?' Kate questioned Sebastian.

'Video games.'

Kate wanted to slap her forehead, but she couldn't do it in front of Sebastian and the entire class. Instead, she slowly shook her head as she logged into her emails and then clicked on the email sent from Mr Winter. She clicked onto the link and a video instantly popped up on her screen. She then looked back at Sebastian and saw him staring at his screen without even blinking. She knew by his reaction that he was not going to survive until the end of the lesson.

'That was an interesting lesson,' said Kate as she and Sebastian made their way to their lockers. 'I learnt something new.'

'I didn't,' Sebastian replied, 'the lesson was just repeating stuff that your uncle spoke about last Friday.'

'If you find the lessons repetitive, why did you choose to do Ancient History?'

'Well, firstly, your uncle's lessons are more exciting than watching videos and doing work. Secondly, someone has to watch your back.'

'You're not wrong there.'

By the time, the two friends reached their lockers, their stomachs were growling loudly. They put away their bags, grabbed some snacks for recess then walked past the noisy crowd of students to sit down at a table that was far away from everyone.

'Thank goodness we have study next,' said Sebastian then took a bite into his chocolate-chip cookie.

'Yes, me too,' Kate replied with a lower voice as she looked down at the top of the table.

'What's wrong?'

Kate stared at the tabletop for a moment before looking back up at Sebastian. 'There's something we need to talk about in study,' she said.

'Uhh...sure.'

'Thanks.'

The two friends continued chattering and eating until the bell rang for class.

They went to the library where students had their study sessions in peace without being distracted by loud noises. Kate and Sebastian sat down at a large table that was shielded by the many bookshelves. Not a single student saw them sitting there.

'So, what do we need to talk about?' Sebastian wanted to know as he pulled his laptop from his bag.

'Well,' said Kate as she rubbed the sides of her arms. 'Me and Samuel visited an art shop yesterday to find my diary and...'

'And?'

'This staff member came up to me and asked if I needed help.'

'And?'

'The woman looks like me but older.'

'What do you mean?'

'She has the same hair and eye colour. Even her beauty was that of a hummingbird. She seemed to know Samuel really well. She tried to hug him!'

'Do you know the woman's name?' Sebastian wanted to know.

'I think it was Summer.'

'Well, if the woman has the same eyes and hair as you, she's most likely your mother.'

Kate instantly froze. She had never ever thought that she had a mother. It had always been only her and Samuel.

'Are you alright?' Sebastian asked Kate.

'T-that can't be right,' said Kate. 'If that woman is my mother, why hasn't Samuel told me about her?'

Sebastian could only shrug his shoulders in response.

'Looks like I'll be having a few words with Samuel later.'

As the two friends grabbed their headphones from their bag, the boys who had mocked Kate's appearance earlier walked up to them with mean smiles on their faces.

'What do you want?' Kate grumbled, knowing that she and Sebastian were about to be hit with a world full of hurtful comments.

'How is a poor girl like you still attending this school?' asked one of the guys with chocolate brown hair that fell down his forehead and over both of his eyebrows.

'What are you talking about?'

'We heard from Mary that you trashed Professor Wood's office and got kicked out of his museum,' said a blond guy.

Have these guys been hit in the head with a bat? Kate thought. 'I don't know what Mary told you, but she's wrong.'

'No. You're wrong. You're ugly and poor and Mary will make sure that the two of you don't show up to school tomorrow,' said the first guy.

With that, the guys walked away, still mocking them. When they no longer saw or heard the group, the two of them looked at each other.

'When will the bullying end?' Sebastian asked Kate.

'I don't know but I hope it ends today,' Kate responded.

They grabbed their headphones from their bags and connected their minds to their own musical world.

The bell rang loudly as the friends made their way to their lockers.

'What have we got after lunch?' Sebastian asked Kate.

'We have English to finish the day,' Kate answered.

'Thank goodness!'

They ate lunch at a table near the canteen. Kate pulled out a peanut-buttered-flavoured sandwich while Sebastian pulled out a small container of green grapes.

'Let's see if we can eat without anyone mocking us,' Kate whispered.

'Hey peasant!' shouted a nearby student, 'your hair looks like a good place for birds to build their nests.'

'Me and my big mouth,' said Kate, ignoring the student's comment.

'Uhh...Kate?' said Sebastian as he pointed to his right.

Mary was walking up to them.

'Oh no!'

'Well, well,' said Mary, with her arms crossed.

The large mob of students suddenly fell silent like the wind as everyone looked at Mary, Kate, and Sebastian.

'I can't believe that a handsome man like Professor Wood didn't kick you out of his museum,' said Mary.

'That's because I'm his niece.'

'Liar!'

Sebastian instantly covered his ears with his hands to shut out Mary's sudden loud voice.

'Everyone knows that Professor Wood is a single man with a loaded bank account!' Mary roared. 'There is no way that an ugly girl like you can be related to him.'

Instead of raising her voice, Kate remained calm. 'Even after you got kicked out of my uncle's museum, you still haven't learnt your lesson, have ya?'

'Did you hear that guys? Peasant girl thinks that I need to learn a lesson.'

Sebastian kept his ears covered as the students laughed like they were cheering at a sporting event.

'The only one here that needs to be taught a lesson is you and weirdo,' said Mary as she leaned closer towards the friends.

'Mary Johnson!' shouted a voice.

The crowd of students suddenly fell silent as Mr Winter stormed up to them.

'Oh no!' said both Kate and Sebastian.

'Mr Winter,' said Mary as she suddenly got nervous, 'uhh...what are you doing here?'

'Go straight to the principal's office now!' Mr Winter ordered Mary.

'B-but why?'

'Now!'

With that, Mary walked through the crowd of students with her head lowered.

When Mr Winter no longer saw Mary, he took a deep breath and then turned his attention towards Kate and Sebastian.

'I'm so sorry about Mary's actions,' Mr Winter apologised to Kate. 'When I saw the email from Professor Wood this morning, I couldn't believe that she tried to frame you for destroying your uncle's books. I'm truly sorry.'

'It's not your fault, sir,' replied Kate, 'Mary can't open her eyes and see that Professor Wood and I are family, even though we look different on the outside.'

'Could you kindly ask your uncle if he can still do lessons with us?'

'I'll see what my uncle says.'

'Thank you so much, Kate, and please, I am truly sorry again.'

With that, Mr Winter made his way out of the canteen.

Kate slowly looked around her and saw the students, realising that she really was the niece of Professor Wood. 'You can take your hands off your ears now,' she said to Sebastian.

Sebastian slowly lowered his hands and realised that the students were all whispering about Kate. 'They're talking about you,' he said.

'I know,' Kate replied.

'Are we going to tell them to stop?'

'We'll stop them if they threaten us.'

'Uhh...okay.'

With that, the two friends went back to eating their lunch without having to worry about being pushed into a deep hole by Mary.

After lunchtime was over, Kate and Sebastian made their way to their last class, which was English. They sat at the front of the room while Mrs Ruby was setting up the projector.

'Hello again, Mrs Ruby,' said Kate.

'Hello again,' replied Mrs Ruby.

'What's today's lesson?' Sebastian asked Mrs Ruby.

'We're going to learn about how to use all the human senses to create a short story,' Mrs Ruby answered.

Kate looked at Sebastian only to find him dropping his head on top of his computer bag. 'I'm guessing this isn't going to be a fun lesson for you,' she said.

Sebastian grumbled and mumbled his sentences, but Kate couldn't understand what he was saying. Instead, she gently patted his back.

By the time three o'clock rolled around, Sebastian and Kate were done learning for the day. Kate said goodbye to Sebastian before getting into her uncle's car.

'How was school?' Samuel asked Kate.

'It was alright,' Kate answered as she put on her seatbelt, 'until Mary showed up.'

'What did she do now?' he asked as he drove out of the school.

'She was about to hurt me and Sebastian but luckily Mr Winter saved us just in time.' Kate then burst into laughter. 'Oh! You should've seen Mary,' she said, 'she acted like the one who was bullied when she was told to go to the principal's office.'

'Sounds like you can finally spread your wings.'

'After three years of constant bullying, yes, I can finally spread my wings.'

'See, I told you, karma would bite Mary in the butt.'

'And it did. Thank goodness.'

Kate and Samuel continued talking all the way home. At home, Kate instantly took a hot shower and then got into her pyjamas. She then went downstairs to find Samuel in the kitchen chopping up the vegetables. She walked up beside him without opening her mouth.

'Are we having vegetables for dinner?' Kate asked.

'Yes, why?' Samuel replied.

'I just have one thing to say.'

'And what would that be?'

Kate immediately wrapped her arms around Samuel's left arm as she rested her head on the side of his arm.

'Hey, what's with the sudden hug?' Samuel asked Kate as he placed the knife down next to the chopping board.

'Thanks, uncle,' replied Kate.

'For what?'

'Thanks for saving me and Sebastian from Mary.'

'All I did was send an email to Mr Winter. I didn't save your lives.'

'But if you hadn't, we'd be featherless ducks now.'

'I'd supposed that's true.'

Kate thanked Samuel again and then unclipped herself from his arm. She then ran upstairs to her bedroom, leaving Samuel alone in the kitchen.

'Thank goodness Mr Winter dealt with that leech,' said Samuel and then went back to chopping the vegetables.

By six o'clock, Kate and Samuel were at the dinner table happily eating the vegetable roast that Samuel had made.

'How was work today?' Kate asked Samuel and then chewed into her carrot.

'Busy as usual,' Samuel answered.

'Not surprised there.'

'Hey, are you alright with Jake picking you up from school tomorrow?'

'Yeah, why?'

'I have an important meeting that I have to attend tomorrow afternoon.'

'Seriously?'

'Yeah, I know. That's why I asked Jake to pick you up.'

'Okay, uncle.'

The two of them went back to eating their dinner. It didn't take long for Kate to stop eating again. 'Hey, uncle?'

'Yes?'

'Me and Sebastian were talking in study about the woman from the art shop.'

'And?'

'He said that the woman could be my mother. Is it true?'

Samuel ignored Kate's question by continuing to eat.

'Is it true that I have a mother that I have never seen or heard my entire life?'

'What makes you think that woman is your mother?'

'She had the same hair and eye colour as me. And she knows you.'

He didn't address her comment. 'Finish your dinner.'

'I want the truth, uncle!' Kate demanded, rising to her feet.

'Don't you raise your voice at me, young lady!' Samuel replied with a louder tone.

'I don't care what you say, you old man! I want the truth!'

'That woman is a snake and you're acting like one too!'

Kate furiously grabbed her glass of half-drunken water and splashed it onto Samuel. 'You're the snake!' she shouted as she slammed the cup down and stormed away from the dinner table.

Kate stormed up the stairs and into her room. She slammed the door behind her, making sure that Samuel heard the loud noise from downstairs.

Samuel quickly rose to his feet. 'Don't you dare come out of your room!' he roared.

'Oh, shut up!' Kate yelled.

Stupid girl, Samuel thought as he grabbed his and Kate's plate and went over to the sink and washed them up in hot soapy water.

'Why am I the one dealing with Kate's problems?' he grumbled as he went back over to the table and grabbed the cups.

'I regret going to that ugly woman's shop,' he continued as he washed up the cups.

After washing up the dishes, Samuel went upstairs to his room and got out of the wet clothes and into dry pyjamas. Even after getting dressed, he still heard Kate's tantrum.

'Keep having a tantrum for all I care. I will never talk about that woman.'

Chapter 11

THE NEXT MORNING, KATE CAME DOWNSTAIRS READY FOR SCHOOL with her head down.

'Morning, Kate,' said Samuel, sitting at the table drinking his protein shake.

'Don't talk to me,' Kate grumbled as she pulled out a box of cereal from the cupboard.

'Are you seriously still angry with me?'

Kate said nothing as she made her breakfast. She ate in silence whilst standing in the kitchen instead of sitting down at the table with Samuel.

It's going to be one of those days, Samuel thought and then went back to his shake.

Once breakfast time was over, Samuel walked over to the sink and filled his cup with cold water. He looked over his shoulder and saw Kate walking away from the kitchen, leaving her dirty bowl on the bench.

'Come back and clean your bowl!' Samuel shouted.

Kate ignored Samuel as she went back upstairs to her bedroom.

Samuel grumbled as he rinsed Kate's dirty bowl, then walked into his library and closed the door behind him.

About ten minutes later, Kate was back downstairs. She collected her lunch and her bags for school then went into the garage to wait inside the car.

Samuel maintained the silence as he placed his own bag and books into the car boot, opened the garage door and got into the car. Samuel looked at her while putting on his seatbelt. Kate immediately turned her head to the window and crossed her arms.

It's going to be a long day for the both of us, Samuel thought.

At school, Samuel parked near the sports hall.

'Have a lovely–' said Samuel only to be cut off by the sound of Kate slamming the door. 'That's just rude,' he said and then drove out of the school.

Why is that man keeping secrets from me? We're family. And family don't keep secrets, Kate thought while looking at the ground.

'Hey, Kate!' said Sebastian.

'Oh, hey, Sebastian,' Kate replied, not even smiling at her friend.

'What's wrong?'

'I...got into a fight with my uncle last night.'

Sebastian's eyes widened in shock. 'You're joking, right?'

Kate shook her head.

Sebastian had never seen or heard Kate fight the man that she had looked up to for most of her life. Even when he visited Kate, he had always seen her and Samuel smiling and heard them laugh.

'Why were you fighting with your uncle?' Sebastian wanted to know as he and Kate made their way to the canteen area.

'You know how we were talking about the woman in study yesterday?'

'Yeah.'

'I tried asking Samuel if she was my mother and let's just say that didn't end so well.'

'Maybe there's a reason why Samuel isn't telling you the truth.'

'Reason? I don't need a reason. I just want the truth.'

Sebastian wanted to reason with Kate but instead, he turned his head away. He spotted a group of female students walking along the footpath whilst talking about Mary being scolded by Mr Winter yesterday. The girls were also talking about Kate being the niece of their favourite history professor.

Have they finally realised that Kate is Samuel's niece? Sebastian thought. *Ugh! Stupid.*

When Kate and Sebastian reached the canteen area, they saw the same group of the popular guys.

'Keep your head down,' Kate whispered to Sebastian.

Sebastian nodded his head and then kept his head down as he followed Kate to their lockers.

Please don't see us, please don't see us, Kate repeated.

Unfortunately for Kate, one of the guys spotted her and Sebastian from the corner of his eye. This was the same boy whose eyebrows were covered by his hair, the one who'd called her "ugly" and "poor".

'Hey guys, look who it is,' said the student.

'OMG! It's her,' said the blonde boy as his eyes followed Kate. 'The niece of Professor Wood.'

'If she's the niece of Professor Wood, how come she's wearing a second-hand uniform?' asked another student.

'Stop it, dude! This is our chance to hang out with a real celebrity kid,' said the first guy.

'Uh...Kate,' said Sebastian.

'I know, I heard them,' Kate replied as she opened her locker door.

'What are you going to do about it?'

'You'll see.'

The two friends placed their bags into their lockers and then closed their doors. They then made their way to Ancient History class with their computer bags. Even when the two of them were quietly walking and minding their own business, students instantly stopped and stared at Kate like she was a walking expensive gemstone.

Everyone was looking and whispering about Kate. Sebastian couldn't handle any more of it, and it was only the first period. He grabbed Kate's hand and sprinted into the classroom.

'Hey guys,' said Mr Winter while writing down important notes on the whiteboard.

'Hey Mr Winter,' said Sebastian. He let go of Kate's hand and sat down in his usual spot in the front row.

Kate went to sit down next to Sebastian only to be called up by Mr Winter.

'Yes, sir?' she said.

'I just wanted to let you know that the principal and I dealt with Mary yesterday,' he said. 'She'll no longer bother you and Sebastian.'

'Thanks, Mr Winter,' Kate replied and then returned to sit beside Sebastian.

As soon as the bell rang, students walked into the room. A couple of the popular boys sat down beside Kate instead of where they normally sat, in the back row with the girls.

What the heck? Kate thought, looking at the pair of boys.

One of the guys waved at her while the other guy blew her quiet kisses.

Seriously? Kate grumbled as she looked at the front of the class. *Why are boys suddenly seeing me like I'm a prized jewel?*

Sebastian saw the boys signalling with their hands and lips. It was like they were trying to gain Kate's attention. 'Whatever you guys are doing to Kate, stop it,' he whispered.

'Whatever,' said one of the boys before he and his friend turned their attention towards Mr Winter.

'Good morning, students,' said Mr Winter as he stood in front of his table. 'Today, we're going to learn about the people of Pompeii and Herculaneum and their lifestyle before the devastating eruption.'

Finally! Something exciting to learn, Kate thought and then looked at Sebastian, who was staring at Mr Winter without even blinking once. She knew by her friend's expression that his brain was going to be fried by the end of the lesson.

Kate was right. By the time the bell rang for morning tea, Sebastian's brain was overloaded like a computer catching on fire.

'I'm officially done learning about volcanoes and ancient cities,' said Sebastian as he and Kate made their way to their lockers.

'Well, get used to it,' Kate responded. 'We have a whole term to learn about the ancient cities.'

'No!' Sebastian grumbled, 'this is worser than ancient Egypt.'

'Worser?' Kate giggled. 'That's not even a word.'

'Please shut up! My brain is fried.'

Worser.

At recess, the friends sat at one of the tables.

'Hey, Kate!' shouted a female student.

Kate saw Mary's large group of female friends all smiling at her instead of laughing and making fun of her as usual. 'What do you want?' Kate asked with annoyance in her voice.

'Come and join us for morning tea,' encouraged one of the girls.

Kate raised her eyebrow. 'Why would I join a bunch of sharks such as yourselves after you all made fun of me?'

The entire group of girls giggled softly while maintaining their fake smiles.

'It... It was a joke,' said another girl.

'Yeah! Plus, Mary was a total jerk,' added another. 'She's not famous like you. She's just a materialistic girl.'

Oh my gosh! Kate thought, shaking her head. 'You want me to join you after finally realising that I'm the niece of a famous history professor?'

The entire group couldn't stop nodding their heads.

'I'm sorry but I don't hang out with people who have ugly souls.'

'What are you talking about?' asked one of the girls sternly.

'Your souls. They are as ugly as the dirt from the earth.'

Sebastian covered his nose and his mouth with his hand to hide his snickering.

'We could've been friends three years ago, but you all chose Mary instead of me,' said Kate, ignoring her friend. 'I'm glad I didn't become friends with sharks.'

With that, Kate turned her attention away from the group and then opened her lunchbox.

Sebastian waited until his laughter had died down before turning his attention to the group of girls. Every one of them walked away with their arms crossed.

'Damn!' he said, looking back at Kate, 'you sure showed them.'

'I had to,' Kate replied as she opened her lunchbox. 'I'm sick of people judging me without even knowing me.'

'And me.'

Yeah.

Kate pulled out from her lunch box a small container full of strawberries. She bit into one and chewed into the red juice like a vampire sucking the blood out of its victim while Sebastian chewed into his chocolate bar.

After three years of constant bullying, Kate and Sebastian were finally able to breathe. Not only that, but they could also finally eat in peace without having to worry about being surrounded by sharks.

After morning tea was over, Kate and Sebastian grabbed their computer bags from their lockers and went to the library. They sat down at the large table that was guarded by the many bookshelves.

'Thank goodness we have peace and quiet until lunchtime,' said Sebastian as he grabbed his headphones and phone from his computer bag.

'Yeah, thank goodness,' Kate replied as she did the same thing. Kate was about to put her headphones in her ears when the boys that badly mocked her yesterday walk up to her and Sebastian's table.

'What do you guys want now?' Kate asked in a neutral tone.

'Me and the boys were wondering if a beautiful girl like you wants to join us for lunch,' said the boy with his hair covering his eyebrows.

Kate wanted to laugh out loud when she heard the word "beautiful" coming out of his mouth. 'And why would I want to join you guys when you made fun of me yesterday?'

'I was joking,' stuttered the student, 'I didn't mean to call you ugly and poor.'

'Can you find it in your heart to forgive us?' asked another student.

Kate looked at Sebastian, who was shaking his head. She then turned her attention back towards the group of students. 'I forgive you,' she said with a smile.

'What?!' said Sebastian, confused.

'Does that mean you'll join us for lunch?' asked the chocolate-haired student.

'Of course,' Kate responded.

'Really?' he said with a huge smile on his face.

'No.'

'And why not?'

'As you said yourself, I'm ugly and poor. Why would I be associating with you when I'm way out of your league?'

The student went to answer but Kate stopped him by putting her hand up in front of her face.

She slowly rose in her spot and then looked at every single boy in the group. 'You only want to be friends with me just because of my uncle's wealth and status,' she said in a stern voice. 'Well, I hate to break it to you, but I will never be friends with those who only see me as a dollar sign and not a person with feelings.'

'Get out of here you ugly and poor people!' Sebastian ordered the group.

The students left Kate and Sebastian alone with their heads lowered.

'For a moment there, I thought you were going to leave me alone to be with a bunch of jerks,' said Sebastian as Kate sat down in her chair.

'I would never leave you behind,' Kate replied.

'Thank goodness,' he said.

Yeah, thank goodness I have that weight lifted from my shoulders, Kate thought and then they both put on their headphones and listened to her favourite songs.

When lunchtime rolled around, Sebastian's stomach growled like thunder. Even Kate heard her friend's stomach growling.

'Man, I'm starving,' said Sebastian as he and Kate opened their lockers to get their lunchboxes.

'Me too,' Kate replied.

'Man, it feels great without having Mary around,' said Kate at their table.

'Yeah,' Sebastian responded. 'I don't know how we survived her bullying.'

'We survived thanks to our friendship.'

'I thought you were going to say your uncle saved us.'

'Well, him too.'

Kate then bit into her sandwich.

'After what happened to us today, are still angry with him?' Sebastian asked Kate before starting his sandwich.

'Well, a little bit.'

'Are you going to apologise to him?'

'Why should I be the one to apologise? He's the one who's hiding something important from me.'

'Hey! If I learnt anything from video games is that some secrets are meant to be kept in the dark.'

Kate wanted to argue with her friend. Even yell at him. But she couldn't, as she knew that Sebastian would turn from a lovable and caring friend to a raging lion in a matter of seconds. Instead, she quietly ate her sandwich.

If only you knew the situation, Kate thought.

'Hey, I was told by my father last night that you'll be staying with us until Samuel picks you up. Why's that?'

'Oh, my uncle has some important meeting this afternoon.'

'Oh! That explains everything.'

After lunch, Kate journeyed to English class while Sebastian went back to the library to have a lesson with one of the specialists who helps him with his autism; they visit Sebastian every three months. The two friends didn't see or talk to each other until three o'clock came around when they were done for the day.

'Is it the weekend yet?' Sebastian grumbled as he and Kate were standing outside the sports hall waiting for his father.

'Nope,' Kate answered.

Sebastian covered his face with his hands and continued to grumble and moan.

Ten minutes later, a small black Kia Rio car pulled up to where the friends were standing. Emerging from the car was Jake.

'Hey guys,' said Jake as he walked up to the boot and opened the lid.

'Hey dad!' said Sebastian as he and Kate placed their bags into the boot. 'How was school?'

'Oh, we'll tell you once we get home,' he said as Jake closed the boot.

'Okay then.'

With that, the trio got into the car and drove away from the school.

Kate put in her headphones into her ears and played music while looking out the window at the passing world for the whole drive to Sebastian's house.

Should I apologise to Samuel? Kate thought, *I mean, he's hiding something so important from me, that's about me, about who my mother is and he will never talk about it.* Kate then let out a soft sigh. *I don't know what to do.*

The trio finally arrived at a small house. Its terracotta-tiled-roof was covered in a blanket of solar panels. Surrounding the house was a tall fence made from wood that cut off the surrounding neighbours.

'Home sweet home,' said Jake as he drove into the garage.

'So, tell me, what happened at school today?' Jake asked the friends once they were inside the house and he and Sebastian unpacked their bags.

'You know how I told you that Mary was scolded by Mr Winter yesterday?' Sebastian explained.

'Yeah?'

'People started talking to us like nothing happened,' Kate said as she sat down on the hard silver stool near the kitchen bench. 'Especially the popular guys.'

'Yeah!' said Sebastian, sitting down on the stool next to Kate. 'They wanted to be friends with Kate even after they bullied her for three years.'

Jake shook his head as he placed his empty lunch container near the sink. 'I'm not surprised,' he said. 'People change their attitudes once they find out that the person they either looked down on or knew is rich or famous.'

'Like Samuel being famous?'

'Yes.'

Jake hung his and Sebastian's bag up on the hooks by the garage door. 'Have I ever told you two about the time people tried to worship Samuel when they found out that he was the famous owner of the Museum of History?'

'No,' said the two friends at the same time.

'Before you two were even born, me and Samuel were having coffee one morning when a group of people wearing expensive business suits came up to us,' Jake explained.

'Just random people?' said Kate.

Jake nodded his head.

Oh boy!

'Anyway, we got chattering away about our jobs and one of the people asked where we worked,' Jake continued. 'Samuel told them about his newly opened museum and let's just say they laughed in our faces.'

Sebastian slapped his forehead while Kate slowly shook her head.

Jake continued to tell the pair how those people had made fun of his friend, claiming that his business would fall faster than a rockslide.

'Did Samuel tell those people off?' Sebastian questioned his father.

'Nope,' Jake responded, 'Samuel simply worked harder and harder over the years until he was finally called to do conferences, speeches and even lessons at schools. His fame and wealth grew quickly. In no time, he had guests visiting his museum every single day. Even women started to admire Samuel.'

'You mean women admire him only for his money,' Kate pointed out.

'Something like that,' Jake replied.

'So, what happened to the people who made fun of Samuel?' Sebastian wanted to know.

'Samuel took all his employees to an expensive restaurant to celebrate the museum's anniversary. The celebration was enjoyable for half of the night until the same group of people who'd made fun of Samuel showed up. You can kind of guess what happened after that,' he said.

'They tried to be friends with Samuel,' Sebastian guessed.

'They got kicked out of the restaurant,' Kate guessed.

'Well, firstly, they asked Samuel to do a history lesson of Night Valley for their company. When Samuel refused, they got down on their hands and knees and begged him to do a lesson. Do you know what Samuel said?'

Both friends shook their heads.

'Bye-bye!'

'That's it?' said Kate with her eyebrow raised.

'Yup,' Jake replied, 'and we never saw them again.'

Then Jake went to the living room that led right off the kitchen, sat on the sofa and then turned on the TV.

'Come on,' said Sebastian, 'let's go and play some video games.'

'Okay,' Kate responded.

With that, Kate followed Sebastian down the hallway and into his room.

Around 5:30pm, there was a knock on the front door. Jake answered it to find Samuel standing patiently in his spot.

'Hey boss,' said Jake. He unlocked the door.

'Evening, Jake,' Samuel replied as he walked inside the house. He couldn't see Kate or Sebastian anywhere. 'Where are the kids?'

'They're playing video games,' Jake answered as he closed the door.

Samuel casually walked down the hallway to Sebastian's room and stood in the middle of the doorway while the friends tapped their fingers away on the controllers like they were running in a race.

'Evening, young gamers,' he joked.

'Hey, Samuel,' said Sebastian, not taking his eyes off the screen.

Kate didn't greet Samuel, nor did she look at him.

'I'll be waiting for you in the living room,' Samuel told Kate and then disappeared from Sebastian's door.

'Great!' said Kate as she paused the game, 'now I have to go home with liar pants.'

'Stop it!' Sebastian snapped. 'You need to apologise to him when you get home.'

'I'll try.'

When Kate got to the living room, Samuel had already picked up her school bags while he was talking to Jake.

'Oh, hi Kate!' said Jake, smiling at the young woman.

'Ready to go?' Samuel asked Kate.

Instead of opening her mouth, Kate walked past the two men and out the front door.

'What's wrong with her?' Jake asked Samuel.

'Cobra,' Samuel whispered.

'No way.'

Samuel nodded his head. 'Yes,' he said, 'I'll ring you later and explain the whole story.'

'Of course! I'll be here.'

Samuel cooked up a quick dinner but Kate didn't eat at the table. Instead, she took her plate into her room and then closed the door behind her. She ate at her desk in total silence. She remained quiet as she took a shower and got into her pyjamas.

She took her dirty plate downstairs, her head bowed low. She didn't look up as she placed her plate beside the sink, where Samuel was doing the dishes, and headed back upstairs.

Samuel stopped her.

'Why are you still upset with me?' Samuel asked Kate.

'You know exactly why,' Kate answered angrily.

'If it's about the woman from the art shop, forget about her. She's nobody.'

'Oh my gosh! Here we go again with the lies.'

'I'm not lying,' he said, walking up to Kate. 'There's a reason why she's better off not being involved with our lives.'

'And what's that reason?' Kate questioned Samuel, crossing her arms.

Samuel instantly froze. His mouth opened but not a single word came out. Only a sigh escaped into the air. 'If I tell you the reason, will you shut up about her?' he said.

Kate nodded her head.

'I'll tell you over the weekend, okay?'

'You better.'

With that, Kate walked up into her room and then slammed the door behind her.

'Damn it!' Samuel shouted.

Chapter 12

Kate let out a giant yawn as she dragged her half-asleep body down the stairs and into the kitchen.

'Morning, Kate,' said Samuel, sitting at the dinner table eating his breakfast.

'Don't talk to me,' Kate grumbled as she grabbed the box of cereal from the cupboard and placed it on the bench.

What did I do now? Samuel thought as he watched Kate grab the milk, spoon and a bowl.

Kate quietly poured the cereal and then the milk into the bowl. She then kept her eyes focused on her bowl as she sat on the other side of the dinner table and silently ate her breakfast.

'Kate?' said Samuel.

'I said don't talk to me!' Kate shouted.

'Look, just hear me out.'

Kate placed her spoon in her bowl and then looked up at Samuel. 'What?'

'I know you still hate me but, why don't we go to the special place today?'

'What's this special place?'

'I can't tell you until you see it for yourself.'

'Are you hiding more things from me?' she asked as she crossed her arms.

Samuel shook his head. 'No.'

Kate thought hard for a couple of minutes until she came up with an answer. 'What are you going to do about school?'

'I'll just tell your teacher that you have a doctor's appointment.'

Kate thought hard again. 'Fine,' she said.

'Great! We'll leave once we're dressed.'

Kate ignored Samuel and his smile as she went back to eating her breakfast.

After the pair finished eating their breakfast, they filled their dirty bowls with water in the sink and then went to their rooms and changed into their casual clothes. They then got into the car and followed the road away from civilization.

Nearly forty minutes later, Kate and Samuel arrived at a small but busy town that was surrounded by the endless blue ocean. The small waves crashed against the cement wall that protected the people as they walked along the footpath. Anyone standing close to the ocean could smell the briny seawater in the air.

'What is this place?' Kate asked Samuel as she and Samuel got out of the car.

'Wellington Point,' Samuel answered.

'Never heard of it.'

'That's because I have never shown you this place.'

The two of them walked to the white-coloured wooden bench that looked out onto the ocean and sat down beside each other.

'So, why is this place so special?' Kate asked Samuel as she crossed her arms.

'I used to come here while I was attending university and watch the ocean,' Samuel answered.

'And?'

'I used to wonder why the ocean obeys the moon's commands.'

'That's because the moon has magical powers. It controls the ocean.'

'Besides the moon having powers, have you really wondered why the ocean never questions the moon's motives?'

Kate shook her head.

'That's because if the ocean questions the moon, life wouldn't exist.'

'So basically, you brought me here just to tell me that the ocean needs to obey the moon to keep life running?'

'I'm saying this because you keep demanding me about the truth about the woman from the art shop when I don't feel comfortable telling you the truth.'

'But you promised to tell the truth over the weekend.'

'I had second thoughts.'

Kate furiously got up onto her feet and looked at Samuel with fire burning in her majestic eyes. 'You're unbelievable!' she shouted, 'I thought I could finally get the truth from your mouth.'

Samuel sat in total silence as Kate continued shouting at him. Seeing her raising her voice at him was like she transformed from a small and fragile hummingbird into a giant powerful fire-breathing dragon. The sight almost made him pour out in tears but managed to hold them back.

'I'm done!' Kate shouted as she stormed away from Samuel.

'Kate!' Samuel yelled as he chased after Kate.

Kate tried to get as far away from Samuel as possible but with his athletic legs, he was able to get in front of her path in a matter of seconds.

'Get out of my way!' Kate ordered Samuel.

'Kate, listen to me,' Samuel replied.

'No!'

Kate pushed Samuel aside and stormed down the footpath.

'Please listen to me,' said Samuel as he hurried beside Kate.

'Leave me alone!'

'Look, the reason why I'm hesitating to tell you the truth is because I'm scared.'

Kate suddenly stopped in her spot. 'What do you mean?' she asked as Samuel stood in front of her.

'If I told you the truth about that woman, I'll lose the little hummingbird that I have raised for years.'

Kate turned her head away from Samuel only to spot him placing his hand on her right shoulder.

'Please Honey Dragon,' said Samuel with a soft voice as tears slowly ran down his cheeks, 'I can't afford to lose the only family that I've got.'

Kate remembered that she was nicknamed after a hummingbird and that they are symbolised for their joy and happiness and that she was not acting like her animal nickname. She was acting more like a hot-tempered phoenix that burned everything in its path. Just thinking about the powerful bird made the anger that burned inside her extinguished quickly. Tears broke out of her eyes like a river.

'I'm...I'm so sorry,' Kate sobbed as she wrapped her arms around Samuel and dropped her head onto his chest.

Samuel wiped his tears and then wrapped his arms around Kate and rubbed her back with his hands. He listened to Kate apologising to him repeatedly.

'It's alright, Honey Dragon, I forgive you,' he said softly and then turned his attention towards the ocean.

I hope that snake doesn't show her ugly face, Samuel thought.

Boy was Samuel wrong.

Chapter 13

The next morning, while Samuel and Kate were having breakfast in their pyjamas, Kate heard Samuel's phone rang loudly on the kitchen bench.

'Your phone's ringing,' said Kate.

'I got it,' Samuel replied.

Kate continued to eat her breakfast in peace while listening to Samuel talking on the phone. The peace didn't last long though.

'I don't know how you got my number, but I don't want you to call me again!' Samuel shouted. 'What? No! You better not show your face or else I'm calling the police. Goodbye!'

With that, Samuel furiously hung up.

'Who was that?' Kate asked Samuel as he sat down at the table.

'Oh, just a scammer,' Samuel answered with his normal tone of voice.

'Uhh...okay.'

The two of them soon went back to eating their breakfast. Once they were done, they went to their rooms to change into their weekend clothes. Kate crossed the bridge and into her studio to organise her canvas and paints for the day.

Kate heard a knock on her door and turned to see Samuel walking into her studio with a glass full of water in his left hand.

'You forgot something,' said Samuel as he handed Kate the glass.

'I was getting there, but thanks,' Kate replied.

'What are you going to paint?' he wanted to know as Kate placed the glass on the table.

'You'll see.'

'Okay, I'll leave you to it.'

After Samuel left, Kate sat down and stared at the blank canvas.

What shall I paint? Kate thought.

Nearly ten minutes later, after endlessly staring at the canvas, an idea popped into Kate's head. She picked up her brush and dunked it into the blue paint. She then waved the brush up and down like a fan onto the canvas until one side of the canvas was completely painted blue. She then mixed a little bit of black paint into her blue paint and brushed up and down on the other side of the canvas.

'There we go,' said Kate as she placed her paintbrush onto the table, 'I just now need to wait until it dries.'

She left her studio and returned to her bedroom and her computer.

An hour later, Kate was in the middle of listening to her music when she heard the front doorbell ringing. She walked out of her room only to find Samuel rushing past her like the wind and down the stairs. She quietly followed him and remained hidden at the bottom as Samuel opened the door.

Kate's jaw dropped to the floor when she saw the familiar woman from the art shop walking into the house wearing a plain pink Bardot top and sky-blue skirt that touched the tips of her fine knees. Her hair flowed down her back and was held in place by a blue flower pin with tiny diamonds that dangled in her hair.

'What the heck are you doing here?!' Samuel shouted at the woman as he slammed the door. 'I told you that I'd call the cops if you showed your face!'

The woman ignored Samuel as she looked around the house. 'The house is still standing,' she said. 'That's a good sign.'

'Stop admiring the house and get out!'

The woman turned around and started arguing with Samuel while keeping a calm tone.

Kate came out from her hiding spot and slowly walked up to the adults without speaking.

'I told you that I didn't want to see your face ever again!' Samuel roared.

'Uncle?' Kate spoke quietly.

The two adults stopped arguing with each other and turned their attention towards Kate.

'Go back upstairs, Kate,' said Samuel.

'Kate,' said the woman, 'my sweet little girl has blossomed into the perfect flower.'

Kate retreated from the woman before she could get her arms around her. 'Who are you?' she asked.

'Sweetie, it's me, Summer – your mother.'

Kate's eyes widen in shock. Her jaw hung open but not a single word came out.

'She's lying, Honey Dragon,' said Samuel.

'Shut your mouth, old man,' replied Summer.

Seriously? What's up with these two calling me "old man"? I'm still young and handsome!

'If you're my mother, how come I have never seen or heard about you?' Kate asked her mother.

'I thought your uncle would've told you. After all, we used to be a couple,' Summer responded.

'Yeah, that was a big mistake!' said Samuel angrily. Samuel then stormed up the stairs to his room and then slammed the door behind him.

'I...I have so many questions,' said Kate, 'I don't know where to start.'

Summer gently pressed her index finger against Kate's lips. 'Save those questions for another day,' she said gently.

Kate slowly nodded her head in response.

'Now tell me, do you like art?' Summer asked Kate as she removed her finger from Kate's lips.

'Like art? I was born an artist,' Kate answered with excitement.

Summer let out a soft giggle. 'Great!' she said. 'Show me your studio.'

Kate walked upstairs with her mother following behind. The two of them crossed the bridge and entered the studio.

'Here's my studio,' said Kate as she sat down on her chair.

Summer slowly walked over to Kate's paintings and knelt in front of the canvases. She looked at each of Kate's pictures. Kate waited silently until her mother was done.

About ten minutes later, Summer got back onto her feet and then walked over to Kate.

'So, do you like my paintings?' Kate asked her mother.

'They're okay, but...' said Summer trailing off.

'But what?'

'You only do the same three styles of painting over and over.'

'I like my styles. I'm comfortable with them,' Kate explained. 'I tried a new style a few years ago, but it gave me a strange feeling. I tried to get rid of it by doing something else, but the strange feeling didn't go away. I stopped trying anything new after that.'

'Uhh...okay,' said Summer uneasy. 'What is your creative mind telling you to paint?'

'I was thinking we could do our zodiac signs,' Kate answered.

'Great!' she said with a smile, 'let me go and grab my art kit from my car.'

Kate watched her mother as she walked out of her studio and disappeared down the stairs.

I don't know why Samuel never told me that I have a mother, she thought. *Or why he wants her gone.*

Summer came back into Kate's studio with a giant black briefcase.

'What's that?' Kate asked her mother.

Summer placed the briefcase on the table and opened it. Kate got up from her chair and peered over her mother's shoulder. Her eyes widened, and her jaw dropped. Inside the case were many paintbrushes, paint sets and other utensils.

'Oh my gosh!' said Kate.

'Pretty cool huh?' replied Summer, 'I always keep a spare kit in the car just in case.'

'I wished I had a kit like yours.'

'I'll buy you one, if you like.'

'Really?' she said with excitement.

'Of course! But first, let's paint.'

After about an hour of roughly sketching their zodiac animals, Kate and Summer walked downstairs to find Samuel in the kitchen making pancakes.

'Man! Those pancakes smell good,' said Kate as she and her mother sat down at the dinner table.

Samuel ignored Kate's compliment and continued to make pancakes.

'Was it something I said?' Kate asked her mother.

Summer shrugged her shoulders. 'Has your uncle ever told you how we first met?' she asked, changing the subject.

'Yeah, at the Broadwater.'

'Oh, man! You should've seen him back then. He would make nearby women drool.'

'They still do.'

'Out of all the women he could've chosen, your uncle fancied me.'

'Shut up!' Samuel shouted.

'Excuse me?' said Summer as she and Kate turned their heads towards Samuel.

'I said shut up!' Samuel snapped at the two women. 'You have been nothing but trouble for the past fifteen years! You shouldn't even be in my house!'

Samuel's sudden loud rage shook Kate's entire body. She burst into tears as she ran from the table, up the stairs and into her room. She slammed the door behind her and threw herself onto her bed. She sobbed into her pillow.

'Kate?' said Samuel.

Kate slowly lifted her wet face from her pillow and saw Samuel standing next to her bed.

'Are you alright, Honey Dragon?' Samuel asked Kate.

Kate turned her head away from Samuel.

Samuel sat down beside Kate on her bed. 'Look, I'm sorry you had to hear that,' he said.

Kate slowly looked back at Samuel. 'Why did you have to shout?'

Samuel let out a sigh as he gently stroked Kate's back. 'I just let out fifteen years' worth of anger from inside me,' he answered.

'Why do you hate her so much?' she asked as she wiped her tears with her hand.

Samuel was about to answer Kate when they heard knocking on the door. Summer entered, put a plate of hot pancakes onto the table along with the fork and a knife, then left without a word.

Samuel walked over to the table, grabbed the utensils and the plate and then walked back over to Kate.

Kate swung her legs over her bed. She didn't speak as Samuel handed her the pancakes and sat back down beside her.

'If you want, we can spend the day at your favourite place,' said Samuel.

'No thanks,' said Kate, eating the pancakes. 'I just want some time to myself.'

Samuel nodded his head. 'Okay.'

Samuel left Kate's room and closed the door behind him.

What is going on with me? Kate wondered. *Why do I get emotional whenever Samuel shouts?*

Questions flooded Kate's mind, but she didn't pay any attention to them. She only focused on eating her lunch while her room was filled with no loud noises. Once she was done eating, she went downstairs only to find Samuel in the kitchen, still arguing with Summer with his arms crossed.

'I told you already! You're not staying overnight in my house!' Samuel roared.

'Please Samuel, I really want to get to know my daughter,' Summer pleaded.

Samuel raised her eyebrow at Summer. 'Daughter?' he said. 'When was the last time you called Kate your "daughter"?'

'Uhh...'

'Just as I thought. Never.'

'What are you two arguing about now?' Kate asked.

The two adults instantly swung their heads around towards Kate.

'Oh, hi sweetie,' said Summer with a fake smile on her face. 'Your uncle and I were just talking about the sleep arrangements tonight.'

Samuel's entire face turned bright red. 'Liar!' he shouted at Summer. 'I never agreed to let you stay over tonight!'

'Come now, my little Scorpio. I know that somewhere in your cold heart that you still love me.'

Samuel clenched his right fist into a tight ball. Almost like he was ready to hit her mother in the face. Kate hurried to place her dirty plate down by the sink and then grabbed hold of Samuel's wrist.

Samuel turned his hot raging face towards Kate.

'Please, whatever you two were arguing about, stop it,' Kate told Samuel.

'But Honey Dragon.'

'I don't care! I want mum to stay with us over the weekend.'

'See, Kate wants me to stay,' said Summer.

Samuel stared at Kate's innocent face and then slowly looked back at Summer. 'Fine,' he said, 'but you better be gone by Monday or else I'm calling the police.'

'Yay!' Summer cheered as she jumped onto Samuel and pressed her soft lips onto his.

After kissing Samuel, Summer sprinted happily out the front door like she had just won the lottery.

'Yuck!' said Samuel as he wiped the woman's kiss off his lips with his left arm.

Kate wrapped Samuel in a hug. 'Thanks for letting mum stay with us,' she said.

He sighed. 'Only because you forced me to agree with you.'

Kate thanked Samuel again and then walked away only to suddenly be pulled back by Samuel.

'Don't get too comfortable around Summer,' Samuel warned Kate. 'She may be sweet and beautiful now, but she will stab you in the back later.'

'Whatever, just let me go,' Kate responded.

'Don't say I didn't warn you.'

Samuel released Kate, walked into his library and closed the door behind him.

'I wonder why Samuel hates mum so much,' said Kate as she went back upstairs to her room.

The giant silver orb in the dark sky shone brighter than the millions of stars. The enormous light shone down on Night Valley like a children's night lamp. Anyone who looks up at the moon is overwhelmed by its mystical love.

Kate, Summer and Samuel were in their pyjamas sitting at the dinner table eating their dinner. The two women were talking to each other while Samuel silently ate his dinner with a bright red face.

'What was it like dating my uncle?' Kate asked her mother.

'He was smart, handsome and mostly protective of me,' Summer answered.

'Did he ever love art?'

'Oh definitely! He used to believe that even the simplest objects can create another dimension.'

'If my uncle fell in love with you, how come you two aren't married?'

'Ahem!' said Samuel, pretending to clear his throat.

The two women turned their heads towards Samuel to find him staring back at them with a scowl.

'I'll explain to you another day,' said Summer, looking away from Samuel and returning to her dinner. Kate resumed eating too.

The atmosphere quickly went from happiness to dead silence in a matter of seconds. The trio didn't look at each other. They didn't speak to each other. All they did was eat their dinner and their forks and knives were the only things making noise.

Once Kate was done eating, she placed her dirty plate beside the other dishes. She retreated to her room, leaving Samuel and Summer to their meal. Kate lay on her bed, staring at her zodiac animal on the ceiling.

'I hope Samuel and my mother get along tomorrow,' she said.

Chapter 14

THE NEXT MORNING, THE BRIGHT AND HAPPY SUNSHINE WASN'T SO bright and happy. The sun rested its giant head on the clouds like one giant pillow and wept thousands of tears down onto the earth.

Kate stood against the glass wall that looked out onto the ocean and watched the rain like she was watching a movie. She often found the rain peaceful; it helped her focus on painting whenever her brain froze up like ice.

'Hey sweetie,' said a familiar voice from behind.

Kate turned around and saw her mother standing behind her. 'Hey, mum,' she said.

'Remember how I said I would buy that briefcase for you?'

'Yeah.'

'I was thinking we could go out and buy it.'

'Like, right now?'

'Yup! And then we can continue with your painting.'

'Ahem!' said another voice.

Samuel was looking back at them with his arms crossed. His annoyed face was at the tipping point of turning red.

'Perhaps we should all go shopping together,' said Summer with a fake smile.

'Can we, uncle?' Kate asked Samuel.

'Whatever,' Samuel answered, 'just as long as the snake here doesn't shower you in gold.'

Kate didn't understand what Samuel meant by that but chose to ignore it anyway.

'Let's go then!' said Summer with excitement as she grabbed her keys and purse from the kitchen and then ran outside into the rain.

Kate made her way towards the front door only to be pulled back by her collar by Samuel.

'What now?' Kate grumbled as she crossed her arms.

'If Summer tries to buy you something else, don't accept it,' said Samuel.

'And why not?'

'She's trying to buy your love!'

'Enough!' Kate shouted. 'I don't want to hear another word from your mouth.'

Kate stormed out, without looking back. She got into her mother's car only to find that the seats matched the red exterior. Her jaw dropped when she turned her attention towards the steering wheel and saw the silver trident.

'No way,' said Kate as she puts on her seatbelt, 'is this car a–?'

'A Maserati Ghibli? You bet it is,' Summer answered. 'I have had this car for a few years now.'

'But how can you afford this car?'

Summer was about to answer Kate when Samuel got into the back seat.

'I'll tell you later,' Summer said to Kate and then drove away.

That's weird, Kate thought. *If mum and Samuel are both wealthy, why aren't they married?*

More and more questions popped into Kate's mind for her mother to answer later.

The trio soon arrived at a gigantic shopping mall. They parked and went inside, out of the rain.

Everywhere Kate looked, she saw people smiling, talking to each other, going in and out of shops of walking around with bags in their hands. The sight of the people smiling was enough to brighten the mall on a cold, rainy day.

'Do you come here often?' Kate asked her mother as she followed Summer up the escalator. Samuel quietly followed.

'Oh definitely!' Summer answered, 'I even come here to do grocery shopping.'

'No, you don't,' Samuel spoke angrily. 'You get the maids to do your shopping.'

'You have maids?' Kate questioned her mother.

'Uhh...yes.'

The trio took the escalators to the top level of the mall.

Kate was instantly blown away by the many expensive-looking shops, including famous brand names. 'No way,' she said, 'I have never seen so many famous brands up close.'

'Really? I thought you–'

'Ahem!' said Samuel, behind Kate.

'Right, right,' Summer replied as she rolled her eyes, 'you two want to live a simple life.'

Five minutes later, they entered into a large shop that was filled with every utensil that an artist could ever want. Kate froze when she saw the number of paint bottles hanging up on the hooks. There were even various sizes and shapes of paintbrushes hanging next to them.

'Are you alright, Kate?' Samuel asked the young girl.

'I'm in heaven,' Kate responded, not taking her eyes off the paint bottles.

'Is she alright?' Summer asked Samuel.

Samuel answered with a stern look. Summer let out a soft sigh as she walked away from the pair.

Kate turned her head to find her mother had disappeared. 'Where did mum go?'

'She's going to look for that briefcase,' Samuel replied. 'While she does, I wanna grab a coffee from downstairs.'

'Why don't we wait for mum? She might want coffee too.'

'No.' He left the art shop, and Kate followed.

'Why do you hate mum so much?' Kate questioned Samuel as they made their way down to the ground level.

'That's something for us to talk about at home,' Samuel replied.

Why is it so hard to get answers from him?

They found a small ground-floor coffee shop that stood in the middle of the mall. There were many people dressed in black clothes either pouring the hot milk into cups, grinding the beans, or fitting the grind into the machine until it drizzled a rich light-brown liquid into the cups. Customers sat at the small brown tables chattering with each other while enjoying their coffee.

'Are you sure this is a good idea?' Kate asked Samuel as they went to the counter. 'You know that women will be staring at you.'

'They can look at me all they want, but I won't be giving them any attention,' Samuel replied.

'H-hi professor,' said a nervous female voice.

Kate and Samuel turned their attention towards the female staff member standing behind the cash register.

'W-what can I get for a strong and handsome man such as yourself today?' the woman asked Samuel.

Samuel ignored her flirty tone and ordered a large flat white coffee with full cream milk.

'Anything else?' the woman asked Samuel, writing the order on her notepad.

'Just the coffee,' Samuel replied.

'Your order won't take long.' The woman then winked at Samuel, confusing Kate.

Samuel, yet again, ignored the woman as he handed her the cash.

'That was just weird,' said Kate as they sat at one of the tables.

'What's weird?'

'That woman, she...'

'Winked at me? Yes, I get that a lot at the museum.'

Kate turned her attention towards her mother, who had appeared behind Samuel. She held a new brown briefcase, a few inches smaller than her own, in her right hand.

'Hi, mum,' said Kate.

'Oh, it's you,' said Samuel, and then looked at Kate.

'I was wondering where you two went,' said Summer. She placed the briefcase beside Kate before sitting down next to her.

'We were just waiting for you.'

Kate shook her head. 'No,' she said, 'uncle just wanted some coffee.'

'Kate!' Samuel grumbled.

Fifteen seconds later, the woman who Samuel ordered from, handed him his coffee. The woman winked at him again and then went back to making more coffees.

Women, Samuel grumbled as he took a sip.

As he did, Kate and Summer spotted the woman's name with a love heart beside it as well as her phone number written on the bottom of the cup.

'How many women have tried to give your uncle their phone number?' Summer asked Kate.

'I lost count,' Kate responded.

'What are you two talking about?' Samuel asked.

'Look at the bottom of your cup,' said Kate.

Samuel lifted the cup just above his nose and saw the message written on the bottom of his cup. 'Sorry lady, but I ain't calling you,' he said and then took another sip.

'It must be a curse,' said Summer.

'What do you mean?' Kate questioned her mother.

Summer explained that she used to be stared at by men from every corner wherever she went. She even had strange men coming up to her, who either gave her their number or attempted to flirt with her.

'Ouch!' said Kate.

'I know,' Summer replied, 'that's why I've hired bodyguards to protect me whenever I leave the house.'

Kate turned her head to Samuel.

'No, I do not need a bodyguard if that's what you're going to ask me,' said Samuel and then took another sip of his coffee.

Kate turned back to her mother. 'What are we going to do now?'

'Now, we're going to finish your painting.'

Great! Samuel grumbled.

Back at the house, Kate continued to add more details to her zodiac animal on the blue painted background to make it look like it had air running in its lungs. Her mother also added more details to her own Capricorn – her zodiac animal, which was a goat with a mermaid's tail – on the dark blue background. After half an hour of constant drawing, the two women took their pencils off the canvas.

'Wow!' said Kate, amazed by the result of the picture.

'I know,' said Summer. 'Who knew that we shared such rare talent?'

'Speaking of talents, where have you been all my life?' she asked as she turned her attention to her mother.

'What do you mean?' Summer questioned Kate as she placed her pencil on the table.

'Why haven't you been in my life since I was born?'

'Well, I...'

'Ahem!' said a voice. An enraged Samuel stormed into the studio.

'Summer!' Samuel roared.

'What did I do now?'

Samuel pulled her up onto her feet. 'Downstairs, now!' he ordered as he pushed Summer towards the door.

Summer stormed out of the studio and down the stairs.

'What's going on, uncle?' Kate asked.

'Go to your room and put your headphones in your ears!' Samuel ordered Kate.

'W-why?'

'Now!'

Puzzled by the situation, Kate walked out of her studio, across the bridge and into her room. She closed the door behind her and then pressed her ear against the door. She carefully listened to Samuel's loud footsteps as he stormed downstairs. When she no longer heard his footsteps, she quietly opened the door and went downstairs, while making sure that she didn't make a single sound with her feet. At the bottom of the stairs, she knelt and listened as the adults argued with each other like two vicious lions.

'I wasn't going to tell Kate!' Summer yelled.

'You were!' Samuel argued, 'I overheard you two talking!'

'First of all, you shouldn't eavesdrop on people, that's rude.'

'I don't care! I've had enough!' he shouted. 'Get out of my house!'

'You can't just tell me to get out of your house right this second. Kate and I are still getting to know each other.'

Samuel crossed his arms as he shook his head. 'You surprise me, Summer, you really do,' he said. 'After fourteen years of no contact, you finally decide to call Kate your daughter. You're pathetic.'

'Look,' said Summer as she placed her hand on Samuel's heart, 'I know that we had troubles in the past, but I know that somewhere in your frozen heart that you still love me and that you can forgive me.'

Kate's jaw dropped to the ground when she saw Samuel shoving her mother off him, nearly causing her to fall onto the floor.

'Why on earth would I still love you when you cheated on me?!' Samuel roared. 'Not only that, but you also left Kate with me when she was only a year old!'

I've had enough of them arguing, Kate thought as she got up and walked over to the adults.

'Please, Samuel, forgive me,' Summer pleaded.

'I have a better idea. Get out of my house!' Samuel roared.

'Enough!' Kate shouted as she stood in front of her mother.

'What are you doing, Kate? I told you to go to your room and put your headphones in your ears!'

'Shut up, uncle!'

Samuel was instantly frozen by Kate's furious voice.

'I can't believe that I was raised by a man who lied to me for years!' Kate shouted.

Samuel was about to open his mouth, but Kate told him to keep his mouth shut.

'This was my chance to get to know the woman that gave birth to me!' Kate continued to shout. 'You, on the other hand, want to get rid of her like she's garbage!'

'She's not your mother.'

'Enough! I've decided to live with mum.'

Samuel's jaw dropped to the floor in horror. His soul nearly floated out of his body like a ghost.

'Is that alright with you, mum?' Kate asked her mother.

'O-of course, sweetie,' Summer replied nervously.

While Samuel remained frozen like a statue, Kate returned to her room and began to pack some of her clothes and utensils into her backpack. After she was done, she walked back downstairs with her bag over her shoulder to find her uncle staring at the ground. His hair covered his eyes.

'Let's go, mum,' said Kate.

Summer glanced at Samuel one last time before taking her car keys and walking out of the house.

Kate walked past Samuel only to be pulled back by her backpack. 'Let me go!' she shouted.

'You're making a huge mistake,' said Samuel as he brushed his hair out of his eyes.

'I said let me go!' Kate demanded as she slapped Samuel's hand, freeing herself from his grip. Kate stared deep into Samuel's eyes, rage burning in her own. 'I'm done with you!' she shouted.

'Honey Dragon,' said Samuel, struggling to hold back his tears.

'Don't you "Honey Dragon" me!' she roared, 'I'm done being your little fragile hummingbird!'

Samuel turned his head away from Kate while tears slowly ran down his warm cheeks.

'You're such a pathetic man!' Kate argued, 'I wish that you weren't my uncle!'

Kate's painful words pierced through Samuel's heart like an arrow. Her words were enough to knock him down onto his knees. Tears ran faster down his face and soaked into his shirt.

Kate could only shake her head as she watched the man crying his eyes out. 'I've had enough,' she responded, 'I never want to see your face ever again.'

With that, Kate walked out of the house without looking back at her uncle. She got into her mother's car and they drove away into the rain.

'Are you sure that you want to live with me?' Summer asked Kate.

'Of course, I do,' Kate replied, 'it's better than living with a snake.'

Summer thought about arguing with Kate, but instead kept her lips closed and focused on her driving while Kate looked out the window at the rain.

After two hours, Kate finally turned her attention towards the windscreen. Her eyes widened almost instantly when she saw the gigantic house that her mother pulled up to. It was twice the size of Samuel's house. It was like she was visiting a royal family. The black metal gate that protected the front of the house was engraved with each zodiac symbol. Guarding the gate were several scary-looking bodyguards.

Summer pressed a button on her keychain to open the gate.

Kate's jaw kept to the floor as her mother drove up the driveway and into the garage that had not two, but three doors.

'Oh my gosh,' Kate spoke when she saw the blue model S Tesla, 'how on earth can you afford two cars?'

'Try three cars,' Summer corrected Kate as she turned off the engine.

Kate turned her head in the other direction and saw an SUV-shaped Porsche painted in an ultraviolet colour. 'Okay, how on earth can you afford three cars?'

'I'll tell you once we're inside.' With that, Summer got out of the car and walked inside the house.

Kate got out, grabbed her backpack and closed the door. She looked at the three expensive cars one last time before walking into the house.

Upon entering, Kate was instantly blown away by the sheer amount of wealth that glittered throughout the building. The stairs that lead up to the first floor had two horses carefully and realistically carved in wood. The walls were full of expensive-looking paintings. The living room area had soft, gigantic sofas that almost looked like beds. The table in the middle of the living room area was held up by four golden dragon-like serpents.

'My goodness,' said Kate as her eyes tried to take in every square inch of the house in seconds.

'Shall I take your bag to your room, miss?' asked a voice.

Kate turned around and saw a slightly older man wearing a black suit and white gloves. 'Who are you?' she asked the man.

'I'm Ben Raven, the butler of this house,' the man introduced himself.

'A butler did you say?'

'Yes, miss.'

Wow!

'Shall I take your bag to your room?'

'Yes, please.'

Kate then pulled her bag off her shoulder and handed it to the butler. After that, she walked over to the kitchen to find several people wearing long black pants, white coats and aprons cooking and cutting food.

How much money does this woman make? Kate wondered as she walked up to the countertop where a female chef was cutting the bacon.

'Excuse me,' said Kate, gaining the woman's attention.

The woman looked up from the cutting board and gasped in surprise. 'My goodness!' she said, 'aren't you Professor Wood's niece?'

'Uhh...yes.'

'Did you say, "Professor Wood's niece"?' asked a male chef while stirring the eggs in the pan.

'Yeah!' said the first chef. 'Isn't this great? We have a celebrity's kid in this house!'

'That's great and all, but what are you guys making?' Kate asked the group.

'Zucchini slice,' answered the woman.

'Kate!' shouted Summer.

Kate turned her attention towards the first floor and saw her mother leaning on the railing.

'Come up here!' said Summer, 'I'll show you your room.'

Kate joined her mother on the first floor.

'Ready to see your room?' Summer asked Kate.

'Yes,' Kate answered.

As soon as Summer opened the door, Kate ran inside the room. She was blown away by this room too. There was a king-sized bed with a small table on either side it, with clear blue vases full of pink roses. A large, flat TV hung on the wall on the other side of the room. The gigantic window gave Kate a view of the trees growing beside the house.

'I feel like I'm staying in a hotel room,' said Kate.

'If you think that's cool, check this out,' Summer replied. Her mother walked up to the wall near the bed and slid it open like it was a door.

'No way! An invisible door,' said Kate as she ran up to her mother's side.

'Have a look inside,' Summer responded with a smile.

Kate walked inside the secret room and immediately ran straight into the bathroom. She gasped in surprise at the black marble steps leading up to the bathtub. An expensive painting of the full moon hovering in the night sky looked down onto the frozen ocean hung on the wall next to the bathtub. The sink beside the bath had a white marble top with golden taps. Kate walked up to the door that was several metres away from the bathtub and saw the shower with two white towels hanging up on the racks on the opposite side of the toilet.

'Impressive, right?' Summer asked Kate as she stood beside the young girl.

'Impressive?' Kate replied. 'How on earth can you live this luxuriously?'

'I'm a famous artist. Plus, I own seven art shops.'

'Famous artist?' she gasped.

Summer smiled as she nodded her head in response.

'I thought you were just a retail worker?'

Summer let out a chuckle. 'You shouldn't judge someone based on their appearance,' she said.

'I know, I know. You sound like Uncle Samuel.'

'Oh please, I don't want to hear that name anymore.'

Kate stared at her mother with her eyebrow raised in confusion.

Summer cleared her throat and then flicked her hair with her hand. 'Sorry,' she apologised with a smile. 'Let me introduce you to River.'

'Who's River?'

'Wait in the bedroom. I'll go and get him.'

With that, Summer left Kate alone.

Who's River? Kate wondered as she wandered back into the bedroom. Kate sat down on the side of the bed and waited for her mother. 'I can't believe that my family is full of famous people,' she said. 'I wonder if my dad is famous as well.'

Kate heard chirping sounds coming from the door. She gasped in surprise when her mother walked into the bedroom with a small, blue-feathered bird with black and white wings on her finger.

'Aww! How cute,' said Kate as her mother sat back down next to her.

'Kate, meet River the budgie,' said Summer.

'He's so adorable.'

'My name is River,' chirped River happily.

'Aww! He spoke.'

'Yup! I taught him to speak,' said Summer as she gently scratched River's head.

'Can I hold him for a bit?'

Summer nodded her head. 'Of course, sweetie,' she said, 'just put your finger out and he'll step onto you.'

Kate held her index finger near River's tiny feet and waited quietly until he finally decided to step onto it. Her heart beat faster, knowing that she had a tamed bird standing on her finger.

'You're so cute,' said Kate.

'Baby bird, baby bird,' said River.

Knock! Knock!

Ben entered the room. 'Lunch is ready ladies,' he said.

'Thanks, Ben,' said Summer. 'Could you get River's food ready?'

'Of course,' Ben said and then left.

River flew onto Summer's shoulder the moment she got up from the bed.

'Let's have lunch and then I'll show you my art collection if you want,' said Summer.

'Thanks, but I just want to spend some time alone this afternoon,' Kate replied as she got up.

'Uhh, okay.'

The two women went downstairs and sat at the dinner table. One of the chefs placed the hot tray of zucchini slice on the table.

'That smells so good,' said Kate.

River flew from Summer's shoulder onto the table.

Kate watched the tiny bird walking past her plate and onto a smaller plate that had a pile of birdseed. *Cute,* she thought.

Summer sliced the hot food into small squares and then gave Kate two of the slices as well as herself. The two women instantly grabbed their forks and ate the freshly made dish.

Kate instantly fell in love with the taste as soon as it entered her mouth. 'It tastes so good.'

'Well, my beautiful chefs always pour love into their cooking,' said Summer.

Kate ignored her mother as she enjoyed her lunch. She kept on eating the delicious slice until her stomach was full.

After the meal, Kate returned to her room and closed the door behind her. She opened the drawer of one of the bedside tables to find a book with colourful butterfly stickers on the cover.

Kate sat down on the bed and opened the book to find several photos of her mother and Samuel as younger adults kissing and hugging each other. She then turned the page to find more photos of Samuel and her mother going on picnic dates and dinner dates.

'Those two made a great couple,' she said, 'I wonder why they aren't married.'

Kate flipped through the book until she came across a photo of what appeared to be a woman with a man standing beside her. Standing in front of the two adults were two young boys.

'Elizabeth Wood, Daniel Wood, James Wood and Takeo,' said Kate, reading the names that were handwritten underneath the photo. 'Who the heck are these people and why does mum have this photo?'

Questions poured into Kate's mind, but she couldn't think of an answer. The only way of getting answers was to get her mother to talk. But she had to wait until tomorrow.

Chapter 15

THE NEXT MORNING, KATE WAS GREETED BY BEN, WHO HAD brought her a breakfast tray.

'Morning, young Kate,' said Ben.

'Morning,' Kate yawned as Ben placed the tray onto the bed. 'Huh? What's this?'

'A bowl of cereal and two slices of toast with hot scrambled eggs on top.'

'I can see that, but why are you giving me breakfast in bed?'

'Your mother wants you to live the best lifestyle, just like her.'

'Uhh...thanks.'

'Enjoy your meal,' said Ben, and then left the room.

'Breakfast in bed,' said Kate as she pulled the tray onto her legs. 'I'm going to love this lifestyle.' Kate picked up the piece of toast with the egg on top and took a bite out of it. 'Mmm...it tastes so good.'

After Kate was full, she got dressed, tied her hair and went downstairs. There, she saw her mother sitting on a chair while a couple of ladies were brushing and styling her hair.

'Hey, sweetie,' said Summer.

'Hey, who are these ladies?' Kate asked her mother.

'This is Taylor and Emily, my hair stylists.'

The two ladies greeted Kate with a smile on their faces and then went back to styling Summer's hair.

'Do you want your hair styled?' Summer asked Kate.

'Uhh...maybe tomorrow,' Kate answered.

'Okay.'

Once Summer's hair was done and sprayed with hair spray, she handed the women the cash from her purse. She then thanked them as they went out the front door.

'Hey, do you have an art studio?' Kate asked her mother.

'I do. Why?'

'Can I look at your collection? I could use some inspiration for my paintings.'

Summer gave Kate a puzzled look, then slapped her forehead. 'I forgot,' she said, 'you're getting settled in my house.'

'Plus, I'm still angry with Samuel.'

'Right.'

Kate followed her mother to the top floor and entered a gigantic room that was filled with paintings. The shelves were full of painting utensils. Small paint puddles on the floor had hardened over time. The walls were filled with motivational quote posters. An easel in the middle of the room had a blank canvas on it.

'This art studio is a mess,' said Kate.

'I know, I know,' Summer responded. 'You'll understand one day when you become famous. Then you won't have time to clean.'

Kate walked up to the paintings that leaned against the wall. She looked at each one until she found a picture of a man with scruffy brown hair and motionless brown eyes. He had the same beard type as Samuel.

'Who's this man?' she asked.

'That's James, your uncle's older brother – and your father,' Summer answered.

'F-father?' she gasped. 'But how? Uncle Samuel never told me that I had a father, or that he had a brother.'

'Hang on a second.'

Summer casually walked out of her studio.

Kate couldn't believe what she just heard. First, she didn't know she had a mother. Now, she had a father that she never knew she had.

A few seconds later, Summer came back with a chair. 'Have a seat,' said Summer as she placed the chair in front of her and then sat down near her canvas.

Kate sat down in front of her mother.

Summer let out a sigh. 'Look, the reason why your uncle hates me so much is because I cheated on him with his brother, James.'

'Why would you break Samuel's heart?' Kate questioned her mother. 'He's everything a woman could ask for.'

'Unfortunately, I was young and stupid back then.'

'Young? You look like you're twenty-five years old.'

Summer let out a soft chuckle. 'I hate to break it to you but I'm actually the same age as Samuel.'

Not bad for a middle-aged woman.

'After your uncle found out about my cheating, he hated me to the point that he wished that I never existed.'

'Ouch!'

'I know. I regretted my actions that day.'

Kate looked at the painting for a second and then looked back at her mother. 'Why does dad look different from Samuel?'

'Your uncle grew up in an orphanage for the first five years of his life. After that, he was adopted into your father's family.'

Kate looked away from her mother.

'Is something wrong, sweetie?'

Kate turned her attention back to her mother. 'I don't know why Uncle Samuel didn't tell me about the existence of my parents.'

'With me cheating on him with his brother, it froze his heart over the years to the point that he wished that we weren't in his life. That's how much he hated us both.'

'I guess that explains why he never talked about you or dad.'

'I know, but your father would take me out on dates every weekend. Unlike your uncle, who gave time to his stupid museum business while I was painting and selling my artworks.'

'Stupid?! That museum is the reason why he's famous today. People love visiting his museum.'

'I know, but I wanted to start a family while I was still young.'

'So, you cheated on uncle with dad just so you could have a family?'

'I didn't want Samuel, a workaholic man, as my future husband.'

'So, why cheat on him?'

'Look, your uncle had little money to his name and I was going to break up with him. But I couldn't bring myself to tell him, as he loved me more than anything else. I didn't want to break his heart.'

Oh my gosh! You cheated on Samuel with dad just because he had little money. Well, too bad that little money turned into big money.

'Anyway, I've ordered you some clothes to try on. They should arrive tomorrow morning.'

'Thanks, Mum.'

Summer got up from her spot and grabbed her canvas. 'Why don't we go outside and do a bit of painting?'

'Actually, I want to practise drawing River.'

Summer nodded her head and then grabbed one of her sketchbooks and a pencil case from the shelf and handed them to Kate.

'River's room is next door,' said Summer.

'Thanks,' Kate replied.

'Make sure you close the door behind you. River tends to fly around the house whenever his door is left open.'

'I will.' With that, Kate walked out of the studio. She went into the next room and immediately closed the door behind her.

Standing in the middle of the room was a tree in a large box with many branches full of different bird toys.

'River!' Kate called out as she approached the tree.

She looked at every branch trying to find the tiny blue bird but couldn't find him.

'River!'

Not even a minute later, Kate felt something pinching onto her right shoulder. She nearly jumped out of her skin when she saw River happily chirping on her shoulder.

'You scared the crap out of me,' said Kate.

River gave Kate several kisses on her cheek and then flew onto one of the branches.

'Cute,' said Kate. She sat down on the hard floor, took a pencil out and began to sketch River.

Kate didn't take her eyes off her picture to look back at River. Not even once. Her hand didn't stop to rest. She kept on going until she had most of the outline of River. She grabbed a blue pencil from the pencil case and coloured in his stomach.

'There,' said Kate as she placed the pencils back into the pencil case.

She looked up to find that River had disappeared from the tree. 'River? Where did you go?'

'Baby bird, baby bird,' said River.

Kate turned her head and saw River walking across the top of his gigantic cage.

'River!' she called out.

River instantly flew over onto Kate's knee.

'What do you think?' Kate asked River, showing him the picture.

River looked at the picture for a moment and then started giving it kisses. 'My name is River,' he said.

'I know that's you. What do you think of it?'

River kissed the drawing again.

Kate let out a soft chuckle as she carefully lifted River up on her finger. For a moment, she watched the little bird chirping and talking. She then remembered that her mother had cheated on Samuel with his older brother.

'There's gotta be a reason why mum cheated on Samuel,' she said. 'Being young and stupid is not an answer.'

'Baby bird, baby bird,' said River.

'I know. I'll just have to keep digging for answers.'

River flew back onto the tree.

'How on earth am I going to find answers?'

An idea suddenly popped into her mind.

Honey Dragon

Chapter 16

THE NEXT MORNING, KATE LOOKED AT EVERY EXPENSIVE-LOOKING shirt and skirt that her mother had brought for her.

'Uncle would kill me if he saw me wearing expensive clothes,' said Kate. 'Then again, he's not here to stop me.'

She tried on one of the shirts. As soon as the material touched her skin, she scratched her back like she had an itchy bite. She quickly took the shirt off and threw it onto the bed.

'Why is that shirt so itchy?'

Kate tried on another shirt only to find herself scratching again. She tried several other shirts until she found one that gently touched her skin and didn't need to scratch. She couldn't help but feel each coloured flower that was carefully stitched onto the shirt.

She slipped into a skirt that matched her flower-patterned shirt and then grabbed the pile of shirts and went to the kitchen to find her mother looking at her phone.

'Hey, mum,' said Kate.

'Oh, hey,' said Summer, looking up from her screen. 'Did you try on the clothes?'

'I tried the shirts and they're itchy.'

Kate dumped the clothes onto the kitchen bench.

'Itchy?' said Summer as she felt the material. 'There's nothing wrong with the material.'

'Well, there is, and it itches my skin.'

'Uhh...okay. I'll return them and get my money back.'

'Hey, I was thinking that we should spend the day doing what actual rich people love to do.'

'And what is that?'

'Shopping.'

'Now you're speaking my language!'

Summer excitedly grabbed her bag and her purse from her room and then went back into the kitchen. 'Which car do we want to take?'

'Porsche.'

Summer yanked the car key from the hook and then disappeared into the garage.

'Wow! I guess mum loves shopping so much,' said Kate as she went into the garage.

Kate got into the car to find her mother tapping her fingers away on her phone. Once she was done, she placed it in the cup holder.

'Before we have fun, let's get some breakfast,' said Summer.

'What are we having for breakfast?' Kate asked.

Before Summer could answer, two tall men dressed in black suits got into the back of her car. 'Hello, gentlemen.'

'Who are they?'

'These are my personal bodyguards. They'll also be looking after you today.'

Lovely.

The two women sat at one of the outside tables at a beach café eating their freshly cooked scrambled eggs.

'What a lovely day to go shopping,' said Kate.

'It is,' Summer replied.

'Do you shop around here?'

'Oh, goodness, no! These shops are for average people, and we aren't average, right?'

'I mean...we could.'

'No! We are what our zodiac signs are; materialistic.'

'True, but–'

'Oh my gosh, sweetie! You need to learn to show off your peacock feathers.'

'Peacock?' she said with confusion.

'Don't you know the symbolism of a peacock?' Summer asked as she took a sip of water.

'I do, but uncle nicknamed me for a hummingbird.'

Summer rolled her eyes. 'Did he seriously nickname you after a fragile bird?'

Kate could only nod her head, which annoyed her mother.

'Well, starting today, you'll be nicknamed for a peacock.'

Kate lowered her head and ate her breakfast.

After the two were done eating, they got back into the car along with the bodyguards and drove further down the coast until they arrived at a gigantic shopping centre.

'Here we are,' said Summer.

Kate remained quiet as she followed her mother into the shopping centre. Her heart started beating faster when she and her mother walked past the crowd of people who glared at them. She overheard the people whispering about her mother's beauty. The whispers mostly came from young men. She wanted to laugh when they thought she was their age when in fact, she was way older than them.

Not one single person noticed Kate walking with Summer. They mostly had eyes on Summer.

I guess people only talk about rich or famous people and not everyday people like me, Kate thought.

Kate quickly forgot about the crowd's comments when she and her mother took the elevator up to the top floor where they found the expensive shops.

'Where do we start?' Kate asked her mother.

'I'll show you where I get my jewellery from,' Summer answered.

The shop they entered had expensive-looking jewellery shielded inside a glass box. Kate's jaw almost dropped at the gemstones shining brightly underneath the light. She couldn't describe how glamorous and surreal each gemstone was, or how they were carefully crafted to tell a story.

They're so beautiful, Kate thought. *Samuel would never allow me to wear real gemstones. Yet again, he's not here to stop me.*

'Morning, Miss Summer,' said a male staff member.

'Morning,' Summer replied.

'Who's this lovely young lady you have with you?' asked a female staff member, standing nearby.

'This is Kate, Professor Wood's niece.'

The man was astonished.

'I didn't know Professor Wood had a niece,' said the female.

'Jennifer!' the man raised his voice. 'I visited the museum several years ago and saw him and his niece opening a new exhibit. Show some respect.'

Finally! Kate thought, *someone finally sees me as Samuel's niece.*

'I'm so sorry about her,' said the man. 'Shall I show you our newest product?'

'Yes, please,' said Summer.

With that, the man walked into the back of the shop.

Kate wandered over to one of the glass counters and instantly spotted a beautiful green pear-shaped gemstone necklace that was surrounded by tiny diamonds.

'Hey, mum,' Kate whispered.

'Yes, sweetie,' Summer replied.

'Can I have that necklace?' she asked, pointing to the necklace.

Summer walked up beside Kate and saw the necklace. 'That's a beautiful gemstone,' she said.

'I know, right. That's why I love emeralds. They're beautiful and they represent the month of May.'

'Do you want the necklace?'

'Yes, please!'

'Can we please have the necklace?' Summer asked the staff member.

The male staff member put on white gloves and carefully pulled out the necklace from the counter into a small purple box, and then into a small bag.

'Thank you,' Kate said to her mother.

'Anytime, sweetie,' Summer responded.

Soon, the man returned to the two ladies with a blue box in his hands.

'What's in the box?' Kate asked the man.

He opened it and Kate's eyes widened when she saw the hairpin. The pin was similar to her mother's but instead of being a blue flower, the flower was filled with tiny red and pink gemstones.

'What do you ladies think?' the man asked the pair.

'It's gorgeous,' said Summer.

'Hang on!' said Kate, 'I thought this was a jewellery shop, not a beauty shop.'

'We sell only these types of hairpins to the rich ladies,' the man explained.

That's so weird.

'We'll take it.'

'Excellent!' the man smiled as he closed the box and took it along with the small bag to the cash register.

After Summer paid for the items, the two women walked out of the shop.

'What do you want to do now?' Kate asked her mother.

'Hang on a second, sweetie,' said Summer as she handed her handbag and the box with the hairpin in it to one of the bodyguards. Summer took the necklace from the bag and placed it around Kate's neck. 'There you go,' she said, 'a beautiful gem for a beautiful flower.'

Kate looked at her necklace for a moment and then back at her mother. 'I don't know why Samuel thinks you'll stab me in the back,' she said, 'I mean, what's his problem?'

'He's trying to stop us from knowing each other. But since he's not here to stop us, we can continue to have fun.'

Buzz! Buzz!

Summer grumbled as she grabbed her phone from her handbag and answered the call. After she was done talking, she sighed as she placed her phone back into her bag. 'Fun time is over.'

'What's going on?' Kate questioned her mother.

'There's a problem at one of my stores that requires my attention.'

'Seriously?'

'I know, but once the problem is solved, we'll go to a nice restaurant for lunch, okay?'

'Yes, mum.'

Kate was looking forward to spending the day doing what actual rich people do. Now, she was forced to wait in her mother's car in the parking lot in front of one of her mother's shops with two bodyguards sitting in the back while her mother went to solve an issue.

So much for shopping all day, Kate thought, watching the clouds slowly crawl across the sky.

Two hours later, Kate spotted her mother walking out of her shop.

'Finally!' she grumbled as her mother got into her seat.

'I'm so sorry,' Summer apologised, 'I keep getting one problem after another.'

'Are all those problems solved?'

'Yes.'

That's when Kate's stomach growled like an animal.

'Perfect timing,' said Kate, 'what's for lunch?'

'You'll see.'

An hour later, Summer and Kate arrived at a large white building that looked out onto the gentle ocean.

'I thought you said we were going to a restaurant?' said Kate.

'We are,' Summer replied, 'just wait until you see the inside.'

Kate rolled her eyes with annoyance as she and her mother got out of the car and went inside the building. The two of them were greeted by the sound of music playing over the radio and the smell of pizza baking in the ovens. The customers happily talked among themselves as they enjoyed their drinks and their food.

'Let's go and sit underneath one of the umbrellas,' said Summer.

'Okay,' Kate replied as she followed her mother.

Kate turned her attention towards the ocean and watched the people swimming in the water. 'Maybe after lunch, we should walk along the beach,' she said.

'Absolutely not,' Summer responded.

'Why not?'

'I hate the feeling of sand in between my toes.'

'You could always wash it off.'

'If I do wash off the sand, my car will get dirty.'

Seriously? She's more worried about dirtying her car than enjoying a simple walk on the beach.

'Good evening, ladies,' said the waiter, 'what would you like to eat?'

'A pepperoni pizza with a cappuccino,' said Summer, 'with full cream milk, please.'

'I'll have a chocolate milkshake,' said Kate.

The waiter wrote down the order on his notepad. 'Anything else?'

'No,' said the pair at the same time.

'Excellent! Your order shouldn't take long,' he said and then left the table.

'What do you want to do instead of walking on the beach?' said Kate.

Summer thought for a moment. 'Actually, we've gotta head home after lunch.'

'Why?'

'I have to get my paintings ready to be delivered to my customers.'

'Can I help?'

Summer shook her head. 'You can practise your drawing with River if you want.'

Kate let out a soft sigh as she looked away from her mother. 'Okay.'

Ten minutes later, the waiter arrived with a tray full of drinks and a steaming hot pizza. He carefully placed the items onto the table and then told the ladies to enjoy the meal before leaving with the empty tray.

'I've been meaning to ask you something,' said Kate and then took a bite into the slice of pizza.

'About what, sweetie?' said Summer as she took a sip of her coffee.

'What was my father like?'

Summer took another sip of her drink. 'To tell you the truth, your father was a jerk and a liar.'

'Seriously?!'

Summer nervously fiddled with her cup. 'While I was in a relationship with your uncle, I met this handsome, tall man while working in my shop.'

Isn't uncle tall and handsome?

'This man, he wasn't like Samuel. He deeply cared about me and nothing else.'

'Uncle was doing the same thing as this man was.'

'I know, I was young back then and didn't know what I was doing.'

'So, what happened next?' she asked, taking another bite of her slice.

'This man, who was your father, started seeing me every time your uncle turned his back.'

Oh my gosh! Kate thought as she listened to her mother blabber on about her father and that he owned a big tech company.

Summer then let out a soft sigh. 'One day, your uncle found me and your father in bed.'

'What did Samuel do?' she asked, taking a sip of her drink.

'He kicked me and your father out quicker than a rocket. I also learnt that day that the man I was dating behind Samuel's back was his older brother and that he wasn't the owner of a company but a regular employee.'

'I guess karma slapped you in the face.'

Summer let out another sigh. 'I know.'

Once Kate's and Summer's stomachs were full, Summer paid for lunch before they headed home. By that time, Kate was exhausted. She instantly dropped onto her bed and stared at the ceiling.

'What a day,' she said, 'I'm glad I got to know more about dad. And mum's cheating.'

Knock! Knock!

As soon as Kate sat up, her mother walked into her room.

'Hey, sweetie,' said Summer.

'Hey, mum,' Kate replied.

'I just want to give you a heads up that I'll be busy packing my paintings this afternoon and tomorrow. So, you can do whatever you want around the house but don't disturb me, okay?'

'Why can't I help you? It will speed up the process.'

'I don't need help!'

Kate's ears rang from her mother's sudden loud tone.

'I'm sorry,' said Summer. 'The frustration is already getting to me.' Then she left.

Kate's tears were slowly building up, but she managed to hold them back.

'She's right. I better not disturb her.'

Chapter 17

THE NEXT MORNING, BEN CAME INTO KATE'S ROOM WITH HOT toast on a tray with strawberry jam on top along with a glass of orange juice.

'Here you go,' said Ben as he placed the tray over Kate's legs.

'Thank you,' said Kate.

'Do you need anything else?'

'My phone, please.'

Ben grabbed Kate's phone from the closet and handed it to her.

'Thanks again,' said Kate.

'Anytime,' Ben replied and then left the room.

Kate went into her messages while drinking the orange juice. She was surprised that she hadn't received any texts from Samuel in the past couple of days.

'I guess ugly face doesn't have the guts to text me. Good riddance.'

Kate dropped the phone beside her and enjoyed eating her breakfast without having to think about Samuel.

After breakfast, she slipped on a shirt with colourful butterflies on them and a blue skirt with white flowers on them.

Knock! Knock!

'Come in,' said Kate.

She was greeted by her mother's hair stylists. 'Oh, morning ladies.'

'What hairstyle would you like to have this morning?' Taylor asked Kate.

'Don't you two need to do my mother's hair?'

'We were supposed to, but she told us to do your hair instead,' Emily explained as she dropped her bag of hair utensils onto the bed.

Kate thought for a moment. 'How about a simple plait?'

'Excellent! I'll go grab a chair from downstairs,' said Taylor and then left the room.

Kate sat on the edge of the bed as she watched Emily lay out the hair utensils on the bed.

A few minutes later, Taylor came back with a chair in one hand and a blue box in the other hand.

'Hey, Emily! Have you got some gloves?' said Taylor as she placed the chair down.

'Yes, I do, why?' Emily questioned Taylor.

'We're gonna need some.'

Taylor then looked at Kate. 'Come and have a seat.'

Kate sat down on the chair while two ladies put on gloves. She glanced over her shoulder and saw one of the ladies taking out the hairpin that her mother had bought yesterday.

'Where did you get that hairpin?'

'Oh, your mother gave it to me while I was coming back to your room,' said Taylor, 'she said she wants you to wear the hairpin.'

'No wonder you need gloves. That hairpin is expensive.'

'It's not just that,' said Taylor, 'your mother said she doesn't want us touching your weird hair.'

Huh? Weird hair?

Kate remained confused as the ladies did her hair.

Why on earth would mum call my hair "weird"? I mean, I have the same hair as her.

A few minutes later, Kate went into the bathroom with Emily and her handheld mirror and saw the finished hairstyle in the mirror. The style was amazing, and the hair clip with its tiny diamonds that dangled like vines sat perfectly in her hair.

'What do you think?' said Emily.

'It's perfect,' Kate replied.

'Would you like the same hairstyle tomorrow?'

'Yes, please.'

'Great! We'll see you tomorrow morning then.'

With that, Kate was left alone in the bathroom. She stared at the mirror for several minutes wondering why her mother thought her very normal hair was weird.

Back into her room, Kate put on her necklace. She then lay down on her bed and played on her phone. A few minutes later, she was interrupted by chirping noises.

Kate looked up from her phone but didn't see anything. She looked back at her phone only to hear chirping noises again. She looked up again and saw a tiny head popping out from behind the TV.

'River?' said Kate, puzzled, 'how on earth did you get out of your room?'

'My name is River,' said River.

Kate let out a chuckle. 'Come down here, River.'

River flew down from the TV and onto Kate's phone.

'I don't know how you escaped your room but I'm glad to see you again.'

'Baby bird, baby bird.'

Knock! Knock!

Kate looked up and saw Ben walking into her room.

'My apologies,' said Ben. 'I was going to give River some food and I... actually left the door open.'

River kissed Kate's screen several times while happily chirping.

'It's alright,' said Kate. 'I'll take him back to his room.'

'Okay,' said Ben, 'I do apologise again for letting River out.'

Kate was left alone with River. 'We better get you back to your room.'

Kate got up with River on her finger and went to his room. She placed him onto one of the branches then walked out only to feel his tiny feet on her shoulder.

'River!' said Kate as she went back into the room.

Kate placed River back onto the branch then left the room again only to feel his tiny feet on her head.

'Why won't you stay in your room?' she said as she placed River back onto the branch. Kate left again. Again, River flew onto her head.

'Fine! If you're going to stay with me, you need to promise me that you'll be a good bird.'

River happily bobbed his head then flew onto Kate's shoulder as she left the room again.

Kate walked around the house until she eventually found her mother's master bedroom.

'Let's see what mum has in her room,' she said as River flew off her shoulder.

Kate walked up to the wall near the bed and saw the many paintings that her mother created. They were mostly landscapes.

'If mum is a famous artist, how come I never heard her name in the media?' Kate wondered.

Crash!

Kate turned around and saw River on her mother's table throwing whatever he could grab with his tiny beak off the table. Mostly her mother's collection of hairpins.

'River,' said Kate as she walked over to River and picked up the pins from the ground.

Kate placed the hairpins back onto the table only for River to throw them back onto the ground. She shook her head with annoyance as she placed the pins into one of the drawers. She was about to close the drawer when her eyes caught sight of a piece of paper folded in half.

Curious, she pulled out the paper and unfolded it.

'Adoption?' she said, puzzled. 'Why would mum want to adopt when she has me?'

Kate looked over at River and saw him giving kisses to a picture of Samuel and her mother.

'Baby bird, baby bird,' said River.

Kate grabbed the photo frame from the table and sat down on the edge of her mother's bed whilst River flew back onto her shoulder.

'I don't understand,' she said, looking at the paper. 'Why does mum want to adopt a child?'

River crawled down Kate's arm and kissed Samuel.

'That does not answer my question.'

River continued to kiss Samuel's face while happily chirping.

Kate dropped the piece of paper onto the bed and then looked at the photo of her uncle and her mother smiling together.

'We could've been a happy family if you hadn't broken Samuel's heart.'

Kate placed the piece of paper back into the draw and then placed the photo onto the table. After that, she took River back to his room and then went back to her room. She spent most of the day watching TV while her mother was busy packing her paintings, ready to be shipped out to her customers.

At end of the day, Kate was at the dinner table quietly eating her dinner with her head lowered.

'What a day,' said Summer as she sat down beside Kate at the table. 'My hands are so sore from packing boxes.'

Kate remained quiet as she ate her dinner.

'Thank goodness all I have to do is take them to the post office tomorrow.'

Kate still didn't acknowledge her mother.

'Hey, what's wrong?'

'Nothing,' Kate mumbled.

'You look a bit upset.'

'I said nothing!'

Summer froze in her chair.

'I'm sorry, mum,' Kate apologised. 'I'm...I'm just tired.'

'Maybe you should lie down and rest.'

Kate nodded her head and then went to her room. She lay on her bed and stared at the ceiling.

'Why?' she said. 'Why does mum have an adoption paper?' She then grumbled. 'Is she thinking about getting me a brother or sister? Or is she...?' Kate sat up. 'Is she trying to replace me? No! She wouldn't do that to her only daughter.'

She then let out a soft sigh as she changed the subject. 'Why do I feel like there's something inside me that causes me to lash out at people? And why does it hate me wearing certain clothes?'

Tiny droplets slowly rolled down her cheeks.

'What's happening to me?'

She went to grab her phone and text Samuel about the sudden outburst but quickly stopped herself.

'No,' she said. 'I don't need Samuel.'

Kate wiped her tears and then rested her head on the pillow.

Don't think about the feeling, Kate thought, *don't think about adoption.*

She then closed her eyes and listened to the wind blowing through the tree outside of her window.

Chapter 18

THE NEXT MORNING, KATE WAS WATCHING A DOCUMENTARY about the ancient pyramids and the pharaohs while eating her cereal in bed.

'This is nice,' she said. 'I can finally relax and watch documentaries without a certain someone opening his mouth.'

Whenever Kate and Samuel watched documentaries together, Samuel would always talk over the presenters and caused Kate to either yell at him to zip his mouth or she would walk out of his room with anger in her eyes.

Once Kate was done eating and the documentary was finished, she got dressed in clothes that didn't itch. By that time, her mother's hair stylists arrived.

'Morning,' said Kate.

'Morning,' said Taylor as she placed the chair down. 'Would you like the same hairstyle?'

'Yes, please,' she said as she sat down in the chair.

Kate turned her head and saw the two ladies putting on their gloves. 'You know you two don't need to wear gloves.'

'Sorry, but it's your mother's order.'

Kate sat in silence while the ladies did her hair.

Once they were done and the clip was in her hair, Kate put on her necklace. She then went upstairs to her mother's studio and found her with a paintbrush in her hand.

'Hey,' said Kate as she walked up to her mother.

'Hey, sweetie,' Summer replied.

'What are you painting?'

'A tree that represents all four seasons.'

'That sounds interesting. Can I help?'

'You help by taking the boxes to my Tesla. I gotta take them to the post office.'

'Uhh...okay.'

Kate took a couple of the rectangle boxes and placed them into her mother's car. She then came back and took another couple of boxes. She kept on moving backwards and forwards until she could no longer fit any more boxes in the car. By then, her arms were ready to fall off.

'Ugh! Is that it?' Kate complained.

'Yes,' Summer answered. 'Until I get more orders.'

Kate looked over her mother's shoulder and saw the rough outline of the tree on the canvas.

'What do you think of it so far?' Summer asked Kate.

'It looks brilliant,' Kate replied. 'I can't wait until you add colour to it.'

'For now, let that dry and once we come back from the post office, it will be ready to add colour.'

Kate followed her mother out of the studio and downstairs. She got into the Tesla and waited for her mother. While she did, she had a quick looked around at the car.

'I can't believe that I'm actually sitting inside an electric car,' said Kate, excitedly. 'This is the best day ever.'

A couple of minutes later, Summer got into her seat. 'Ready to go?' she asked.

'Yes.'

With that, the two women drove away from the house.

A couple of hours later of constant driving on the road, the two women finally arrived at the post office.

'Do you want to wait in the car?' Summer asked Kate.

'Yeah,' said Kate. 'I'll be fine here.'

'Okay.'

Summer closed her door and walked into the post office.

Kate looked out the window at the trees and instantly spotted a couple of birds with pink stomachs, a grey back and a white head sitting on a branch happily chirping and making other loud noises.

'Aww!' said Kate. 'They are so cute.'

The pink-feathered birds that were sitting in the tree were common galahs or rose-breasted cockatoo, another native species of Night Valley. They were known to be noisy but cute birds. Kate used to see the birds make loud noises in the tree near Samuel's house in the morning when she was younger. She remembered Samuel waking up in a grumpy mood every time the galahs visited the house. One day, they had a ferocious storm. The wind was so strong that it knocked over the tree, like dominos falling in a line. Since then, Kate could only see her feathered friends whenever she and Samuel spent time together.

Ten minutes later, Kate heard the boot opening. Summer and one of the post office employees carefully took all the boxes out of the car and put them into a shopping trolley. Once there were no more boxes in the back, Summer closed the boot and they went back inside the post office.

Kate looked back at her bird friends only to watch them fly away into the distance.

'Aww!' Kate said, disappointed.

Fifteen minutes later, Summer arrived back. 'Thank goodness that's done,' she said as she put on her seatbelt.

'Why does it take so long just to deliver packages?'

'The employees needed to make sure that I wasn't sending anything illegal, like drugs.'

'If you did have any drugs, you would be in jail by now.'

Summer let out a chuckle. 'That's why it's better to have a clean and healthy lifestyle.'

'Speaking of lifestyles,' she said as her mother drove away from the post office, 'with the cars you have, why didn't you get a Lamborghini or a Ferrari even?'

'I used to own a Ferrari before I met your uncle. Until someone spray-painted "gold digger" on the side and smashed the windows.'

'Ouch!'

'I know! I worked hard and saved up money on my own to get a Ferrari until some jealous person came along and destroyed my dream car.'

'What about a Lambo?'

'Some guy tried to steal my car once. So, I had to sell it and get a Tesla instead.'

Kate shook her head. 'That has happened a couple of times with Samuel.'

'What has?'

'I remember Samuel telling me that ladies would wait by his car every time he finished work and would flirt with him until he decided to go out with one of them.'

'Did he fall for any of those women?'

'Of course not! He knows that they are only after his money and not his feelings.'

Summer rolled her eyes. 'Samuel had always had thick skin when it came to women and their attempts to win his heart.'

'He once told me that if he does get married one day, he wants a woman who loves him for his heart and not for the amount of money he has.'

Summer slowly nodded.

Two hours later, the pair finally arrived home. Summer went to her studio while Kate sat beside her, watching her paint in the tree.

'Are you going to use the fan brush for the leaves?' Kate asked her mother.

'I will in a minute,' said Summer. 'Don't rush me.'

'Let me help you with that,' Kate said as she grabbed the brush.

'Put that down!'

Kate was almost brought to tears by her mother's sudden loud voice.

Summer took a deep breath. 'I-I'm sorry sweetie,' she said as she took the brush from Kate's hand. 'Just leave me alone while I paint.'

Confused, Kate left the art studio and went to River's room.

'That was weird,' said Kate. 'Why did mum suddenly shout at me?'

'Baby bird, baby bird,' said River.

Kate turned her head and saw River in his cage kissing himself in the mirror. She sat down on the hard floor before calling River. River immediately crawled out of his cage and flew onto Kate's knee.

'Thank goodness you're in a happy mood,' said Kate as she stroked River's head with her finger.

'Baby bird, baby bird,' said River.

'That's right. You're always happy to see me.'

After stroking River's little fluffy head, the tiny bird crawled down Kate's leg and hopped onto the floor.

'That's strange,' said Kate. 'Why would mum suddenly shout at me when I did nothing wrong?'

River kissed the side of Kate's leg, making her laugh. 'Stop it!' Kate laughed.

River instantly stopped and then flew onto the tree.

Once Kate was done laughing, she got up to her feet.

'Thanks for making me laugh, River,' she said and then left the room.

Kate went back to her room and then closed the door behind her. She sat on the edge of the bed and took out the photo album. She passed the time by looking at each and individual photo of her uncle and her mother.

Knock! Knock!

Kate quickly closed the book and placed it back into the drawer. 'Come in!'

'Hey, sweetie,' said Summer softly.

'Oh, hi.'

'I'm sorry that I yelled at you earlier. I was so busy concentrating on my picture that I accidentally hurt your feelings.'

'I do that sometimes when something or someone distracts me from painting.'

'Are you okay now?' she asked as she sat down beside Kate.

'I'm okay. River cheered me up.'

'Would you like some lunch?'

'Yes, please.'

'Let's go then.'

The two women went downstairs. At the dinner table, one of the chefs handed them plates of steak and chips with tomato sauce on top. Another chef gave them each a glass of water and their forks and knives.

'Let's eat,' said Summer.

They ate their steak while happily talking to each other. Midway through lunch, Summer left the table.

'Where are you going?' Kate asked her mother.

'I...forgot something from my art studio,' Summer answered. 'I'll be back in a minute.'

Okay, Kate thought as she went back to eating her lunch.

After Kate was done eating, she left the table and went to her mother's studio. For some reason, the door of the studio was closed.

'That's weird,' said Kate. 'Why does mum have her door shut?'

Kate went to open the door only to stop herself when she heard her mother talking over the phone. She pressed her ear against to the door and listened to the conversation.

'I can't believe that kid fell for the story that I cheated on Samuel with his older brother,' Summer laughed. 'I mean really. I never loved Samuel from the beginning.'

Kate covered her mouth with her hand in shock. *I never thought I would hear a woman hate Samuel.*

'Like seriously, why on earth would Samuel want to raise a teenager that has a disease? If I was him, I would get rid of her and have normal children.'

Huh? Disease?

'I thought by now that Kate would be cured. But no. She still has it.'

What on earth is mum talking about? I'm healthy as ten girls.

'I can't believe that I thought she was the perfect flower. Ugh! She's a broken and useless child!'

Kate felt an arrow piercing her heart. Tears instantly ran down her cheeks like a river. She had never heard such toxic words about her.

'I know, I know. Once you're out, I'll hand that weird kid back to Samuel and we'll adopt a normal child.'

Kate cried as she sprinted back to her room. She then slammed the door, grabbed her phone and rang Samuel.

'Please uncle, pick up,' Kate sobbed.

No matter how many times Kate wiped her tears, they keep on pouring out.

'Pick up the phone, uncle.'

A few minutes later, Kate heard Samuel's voice.

'What can I do for you stranger?' he said.

'Take me home!' Kate pleaded.

'Why would I take you home? I thought you were loving the elite lifestyle?'

'Please, uncle!'

'Why would I when someone doesn't want to see my face ever again?'

'I'm sorry, uncle.'

'Nah! I think you and your mother are better off living together.'

'You don't understand. Mum said I have some disease and that she was going to adopt a normal kid.'

Samuel went silent.

'Pack your bag. I'll be there in a couple of hours.'

Kate wiped her tears as she grabbed her bag from the closet and began putting her items into her bag. She took the photo of the family from the album and put it into her bag.

Knock! Knock!

'Open the door right now!' shouted Samuel.

Kate went downstairs to find her mother running to the front door. She opened the door only to be pushed back by Samuel.

'W-what are you doing here? And how did you get past my security guards?' Summer asked as he walked inside.

'You shouldn't be worrying about your security guards. You should be worried about yourself.'

'Uncle!' Kate cried as she ran up to Samuel and tightly wrapped her arms around him.

'Are you alright, Honey Dragon?' Samuel asked Kate gently.

'After what mum said about me, no.'

Samuel looked at Summer with rage in his eyes. 'I'm not surprised.'

'What are you two talking about?' said Summer.

'Quit the act, Summer. Kate told me everything over the phone.'

'So what? It's all true.'

'Why are you so mean?' Kate sobbed.

'How dare you!' Samuel roared as he walked up to Summer. 'Why do you keep treating your own flesh and blood like garbage?'

Summer furiously crossed her arms. 'Well, she is garbage and I intend returning her to you.'

'You've been so selfish ever since she was diagnosed with autism.'

A-autism? Kate puzzled.

Summer turned her head away from Samuel.

'Tell me, Summer, why were you trying to get back together with me?' said Samuel.

'I thought that Kate would be cured by now,' she said, looking back at Samuel.

Samuel slapped his forehead. 'Are you that stupid? Autism doesn't magically go away overnight. It's a lifelong disorder.'

'Whatever! Just get that weird girl out of my sight.'

Samuel angrily clenched his fists. 'Are you seriously just going to abandon your daughter again?'

'Yes, and I don't care. I didn't ask for a broken girl.'

Tears continued to run down Kate's cheeks. The words that came from her mother's mouth were like poison from a snake's fangs. They weren't sweet like nectar from a flower.

Samuel looked back at Kate and saw her staring at the ground with tears soaking her shirt. He walked back to Kate and wrapped his arms around her.

Kate's tears poured out onto Samuel's shirt, but he didn't care.

'You know what, Summer? Kate and I are better off without you,' he said. 'We don't need another woman in our lives. We especially don't need a woman who treats others differently.' Samuel gently rubbed Kate's head. 'Let's go home.'

Kate slowly nodded.

'That's right! Get out of here!' Summer shouted. 'I'll adopt a child and when I do, I will make sure he or she isn't broken.'

Samuel stopped in the doorway. 'Sure!' he said as he looked back at Summer. 'Go ahead and adopt a child. I'll just tell them that you abandoned your daughter on my doorstep fourteen years ago.'

Summer instantly froze in her spot.

'That's what I thought. You're afraid to lose your ego and status if I spill the beans.'

Samuel and Kate went to the car only to be stopped by Summer.

'Please don't tell anyone,' Summer pleaded Samuel. 'All I ever wanted was to be a mother.'

Samuel crossed his arms. 'You could've been a mother if you haven't left Kate with me all those years ago.'

Summer fell silent as she cried.

'Just as I thought.' Samuel then turned to Kate. 'Get in the car, Honey Dragon.'

Kate wiped her tears and then got into Samuel's car.

'Don't you ever show your vulture face ever again!' Samuel warned Summer. 'If I ever see you or if you attempt to talk to Kate, I will call the police. Got it?'

Summer nodded her head.

With that, Samuel got into his car and drove away. Leaving Summer alone.

Back at the house, Kate stood near the kitchen bench with her gaze lowered to the floor while Samuel took off her necklace and the hairpin from her hair.

'There we go,' said Samuel as he threw the items into the bin underneath the sink.

Kate said nothing as she wiped her tears.

'Once you get out of those clothes, we'll throw them into the bin.'

Kate still said nothing.

'Honey Dragon?'

Kate slowly looked up at Samuel. 'You lied to me.'

'Excuse me?'

'Why would I be autistic when I'm completely normal?! And what's the thing about mum abandoning me on your doorstep?'

Samuel let out a deep sigh. 'Let's go to your room. We'll talk there.'

Kate went to her room with Samuel following. They sat down on the edge of her bed.

'Start explaining,' said Kate as she dumped her bag onto the floor.

Samuel nervously rubbed the side of his arms. 'When you were born, you were a completely healthy child. Your mother loved to spend time with you, so I rarely had the chance to hold you,' Samuel explained and then let out a chuckle. 'I remember the time that you sucked on my nipple trying to get milk out of me.'

Kate let out a weak chuckle.

'When you turned a year old, I was babysitting you for a day while your mother worked on her painting. I went to hug you but for some reason, you didn't want to be hugged. Sometimes, I would find you staring at the fridge.'

'I don't remember doing that.'

'You were only a year old,' Samuel pointed out. 'Anyway, I asked Jake, and he said it was autism. I didn't believe him, so I took you to see a doctor and...he said you have autism.'

'What did mum say when she found out?'

Samuel shook his head. 'She stopped spending time with you.'

Kate's eyes widened in shock.

'A couple of months later, I found you on my doorstep all alone.'

Kate wiped her tears.

'I rang your mother and asked her why she left you on my doorstep. She told me that she didn't want to be seen with a kid that has a disease and that she never wanted to see your face ever again.'

'No...' she sobbed into her hands.

Samuel wrapped his arm around Kate and gently stroked her arm, but Kate shoved his arm off her.

'Stop touching me!' Kate shouted as she stood up in front of him. 'You're going to abandon me as mum did to me!'

'What nonsense are you talking about?'

'You're going to get rid of me, aren't you? I bet that's why you've been nice to me for years. You're probably only doing that so that you can't get rid of me, a broken girl.'

Samuel shook his head as he muttered something in Japanese.

'Who was there when you fell?' he asked in English.

'You,' Kate answered.

'Who was there when you were sick?'

'You.'

'Who was there to take you to the beach?'

'You.'

'Who was there to give you food and a roof over your head?'

'You.'

'See, would I abandon the hummingbird that I have been raising for years?'

Kate wiped her tears and then shook her head. She then sat back down beside Samuel but kept her head lowered. 'Why didn't you tell me that I had autism?'

'Because I don't see an autistic person. All I see is Kate Summer – the Honey Dragon.'

Kate looked up at Samuel. 'What?'

Samuel wrapped his arm around Kate. 'Before I owned a museum, I used to have a good friend who lost both of his legs in a car accident. People made fun of him because he had prosthetic legs. I did my best to protect him, but it wasn't enough. He...he committed suicide a few weeks later.'

Kate saw the wet tears breaking out of Samuel's eyes.

'Why couldn't people look past those legs?' Samuel complained as he wiped his tears. 'Why couldn't they see that he was still human?'

'I'm sorry.'

Samuel wiped his tears again and then took a deep breath.

'Going back to my question from earlier; why was I nicknamed after a hummingbird?'

'Well, I knew that the moment you were born, a fragile but strong hummingbird had been born inside you.'

Kate wiped her tears with her hand.

'Remember that day when the man threatened me?'

Kate nodded in response.

'Your little hummingbird spirit saved me. Thank you.'

'I...guess I did.'

Samuel leaned in and kissed Kate's forehead.

'Oh! I remembered something.' Kate opened her bag and pulled out the photo of the people. 'I was going through mum's album a few days ago and found this picture,' she said as she handed Samuel the photo. 'Do you know who these people are?'

Samuel looked at the photo for several minutes and then sighed sadly.

'Did your mother ever tell you about my childhood?' he asked.

'She said you used to live in an orphanage and then was adopted into my dad's family.'

'The two adults in this photo are my adoptive parents and your grandparents.'

'And the two boys?'

'James and Takeo, which is me.'

Kate's jaw dropped to the ground. 'Your real name is Takeo?'

Samuel nodded his head. 'I was given the same Samuel Wood when I was adopted and came to Night Valley. Ever since then, I have always been called Samuel.'

'So...do I call you uncle Samuel or uncle Takeo?'

'Call me what you've always been calling me.'

'Okay, Uncle Takeo.'

Samuel raised his eyebrow.

'I'm just joking,' she laughed, making Samuel roll his eyes with annoyance.

Girls.

'Do you remember anything from your childhood when you were living in Japan? Like your last name? Anything?'

Samuel shook his head. 'Nothing.'

Kate covered her mouth in shock. 'Nothing?'

'Nothing.'

Oh my gosh, she thought.

Kate felt her tears slowly building up but managed to hold them back. She could have never imagined anyone like Samuel to not remember their own name or even the country they grew up in.

'How did you survive all those years in Night Valley?' she asked.

'All I did was follow my heart and my passion for history.'

'And here you are, a famous history professor.'

'And I own a museum.'

Kate nodded her head and then changed the subject.

'I just have one more question,' she said.

'What is it?'

'Where's dad?'

Samuel patted Kate's back. 'He's currently doing time behind bars.'

'Oh.'

'But don't worry about him. He will never show his face in front of us.'

Kate felt relieved when she heard those words. 'Just one more thing,' she said.

'Yes, Honey Dragon?' Samuel replied.

'When mum said she was kicked out of the house by you, whatever happened to her after that?'

Samuel paused for a moment.

'After I kicked out your mother, she came back to me a month later saying she was pregnant and that she wanted to stay with me,' he explained. 'I told her to go back to her lover, but she said that he got into trouble with the law and needed me to help her out with the baby.'

'Did you help her?' said Kate.

'Even though I hated your mother for cheating on me, I had no choice but to help her.'

'Did you ever do *it* with mum before she cheated on you?'

'What do you mean?'

'I mean, have you ever done the adult thingy with mum?'

'Why do you think that I'm a virgin?'

'I was just checking so that I know that I'm your niece and not your daughter.'

'You would've been my daughter if your mother hadn't cheated on me.'

Yeah.

Kate then lowered her head. 'I owe you a sincere apology, uncle.'

'You don't need to apologise, Honey Dragon.'

'Yes, I do,' she said, looking back up at Samuel. 'I have been pressuring you into telling me about your ex-girlfriend when you didn't want to. You even tried to protect me from mum when I was only interested in learning more about her.' Tears ran down Kate's cheeks. 'I should've listened to you in the beginning.'

Samuel wrapped his arm around Kate and rubbed the side of her arm. 'It's not your fault,' he responded. 'A part of this is my fault.'

'What?' she cried.

'I should've told you that you had a mother. Yet again, I couldn't tell you because I was afraid to tell you that your mother abandoned you, all because you're autistic.'

Kate wiped her tears with her hand. 'Why didn't you abandon me when you found out that I'm autistic?'

'Because I loved you even before you were diagnosed, and I will never stop loving you.' Samuel then gently wiped Kate's remaining tears with his thumb as she smiled back at him.

'There's something that I need to do,' said Kate as she got up onto her feet.

'Like what?' he asked.

'You'll see.'

Kate walked out of her room, across the bridge and into her studio. She grabbed the canvas that she and her mother did and then walked out of her studio. She went across the bridge only to stop in the middle.

She looked at the painting without paying attention to Samuel, who walked up to her.

For a minute, the two of them kept their mouths shut until Kate broke the silence that filled the house.

'It's such a shame,' said Kate. 'Me and mum would've gotten along with each other if only she looked past my disability.'

'She's never going to change,' Samuel replied.

'I know.'

With that, Kate threw the painting over the railing. The canvas broke on the hard floor. Kate and Samuel looked over the railing at the pieces.

'I thought you were going to keep that painting,' said Samuel.

'Nah!' Kate replied. 'I didn't like mum's drawing. Besides, she forgot to add more details to her zodiac animal.'

The two of them walked downstairs and picked up the broken canvas. They then walked out the front door and placed the pieces into the garbage bin that stood beside the house.

'From now on, I will be the only one doing the painting,' said Kate. 'I don't need a selfish mother to change my art style. All I need is my imagination and a paintbrush.'

'And my support,' Samuel added.

'That too.'

The two of them went back inside the house a grabbed a bottle of water from the fridge.

'Hey, uncle, I forgot to ask, why is dad behind bars?' Kate wanted to know.

'After your father lost his job, he turned to drugs,' Samuel answered and then took a sip of water.

'Why wouldn't dad find another job instead of turning to the evil side?'

Samuel shrugged.

'Does he know that I'm his daughter?'

'I sent your father a photo of you when you were a baby and a letter but I never, ever got a response from him,' Samuel replied.

'What about now?'

'Nope.'

'Is there a reason for that?'

'Maybe back then he wasn't ready to be a father; or maybe he doesn't care, like your mother. Who knows?'

'Oh,' she said.

'Don't worry though. We have plenty of time before he gets out of prison.'

'Whatever you say, uncle.'

They drank their water in silence for a moment, only to be interrupted by the sound of Samuel's phone. Samuel answered it.

'Hey Jake,' said Samuel.

'Hey, boss! I got some good news,' Jake replied.

'What's the good news?'

'I tell you tomorrow in person.'

'Why can't you just tell me over the phone?'

'It wouldn't be exciting then.'

Samuel rolled his eyes. 'I'll be home tomorrow.'

'Great! I'll see you tomorrow boss.'

With that, Jake hung up.

'What did Jake have to say?' Kate asked.

'He'll be coming over tomorrow to tell me some good news,' Samuel responded.

'Why couldn't he just tell you over the phone?'

'I asked the same thing but no, he'd rather tell me in person.'

'The news better be worth it.'

'I hope so too.'

Chapter 19

THE NEXT MORNING, THE SUN HAPPILY SMILED DOWN ON THE earth. There was not a single cloud in the sky to hide the sun's smile.

Kate and Samuel happily chattered at the dinner table while eating their cereal.

'What a nice day to paint,' said Kate.

'If Sebastian is coming over, you could paint with him,' Samuel replied.

'Actually, Sebastian and I are going to have a special talk.'

'What's this special talk that you're going to have with him?'

'I think you know the answer to that, uncle.'

Samuel thought for a moment while he chewed his cereal. 'No, not really.'

'It starts with an "a" and ends with an "m".'

Samuel thought again until a lightbulb lit up in his head. 'Oh, that.'

'Yes, that.'

'Well, I'll leave you and Sebastian alone while Jake and I talk about adult stuff.'

'Thanks, uncle.'

Once the pair was done eating, they cleaned up their dirty bowls and then went to their rooms and got dressed. Then they heard knocking on the door.

'That's probably them now,' said Samuel, going to answer it.

Jake and Sebastian greeted Samuel as they walked inside the house.

'Morning Kate,' said Sebastian.

'Morning Sebastian,' Kate replied with a smile.

'Okay,' Samuel said to Jake. 'What's the good news you need to tell me?'

'Well, Sebastian and I were watching the news yesterday when we saw a familiar face on TV,' Jake explained.

'And whose face was it?'

'Mr Johnson.'

'You're joking, right?' said Kate.

'Nope.'

'What did he do now?' Samuel questioned his friend. 'Buy some poor business and is planning on turning it into a casino?'

'Nope.'

'What did he do?'

'He got arrested by the police.'

Kate and Samuel's jaws dropped with surprise.

'You're kidding,' said Samuel.

'Nope,' Jake replied. 'Turns out that his wealthy lifestyle that we all thought that he had was the result of him scamming people and embezzlement.'

'So, all this time, Mary thought she was better than everyone else because she was rich. She turns out to be a common person,' said Kate.

'If only she came back to school,' said Sebastian. 'Oh! I would love to see her be the target of bullying.'

'That doesn't matter now. She's probably going to another private high school.'

'Actually, Mary won't be going to any school,' Jake pointed out. 'The police got hold of every dollar that Mr Johnson stole from people. So, Mary won't be going to any school for a while.'

Finally! Kate thought. *I can finally focus on schoolwork without having Mary bully me.*

Kate was not only happy that she no longer had to deal with the biggest bully in her life, but Sebastian could somewhat breathe without Mary making fun of him.

'With Mr Johnson out of the picture, he can no longer touch the museum with his greedy hands,' Jake continued.

'See Kate, I told you that Mr Johnson's thirst for money would be his downfall,' Samuel said to Kate.

'And you were right,' Kate replied. 'Again.'

'Anyway,' he said, looking back at his friend. 'You and I need to have a chat in my office.'

'About what?' Jake questioned Samuel.

'Just follow me.'

Jake followed his friend upstairs.

'I hope dad isn't in trouble with Samuel,' said Sebastian.

'Don't worry about him,' Kate replied. 'Let's just go outside and watch the ocean.'

Sebastian nodded and then followed his friend outside, where they sat down on the pool chair.

For a while, the two friends sat in silence and watched the birds flying over the quiet, still water. They paid no attention to the wind as it blew gently through their hair.

'Isn't the ocean beautiful today?' Kate asked, breaking the silence.

'Yes,' Sebastian answered. 'Although, I prefer to touch the water at the beach.'

'I guess that's true.'

The two friends fell quiet again.

Should I tell him or not? Kate thought, watching the ocean. *If I don't tell him, he might think that he's the only one with autism. Come on brain! Do something.*

'Hey, Sebastian.'

'Yes?'

'I know this might sound personal but, do you have a mother?'

'Say again?' he said, looking at his friend.

'I know it had always been you and Jake but, do you have a mother?'

'And why are you asking me this?'

'Well, I...I'm curious.'

Sebastian thought for a minute.

'I mean, if you don't want to answer, that's fine.'

'Dad told me that she died from complications after I was born,' Sebastian answered.

Kate covered her mouth in shock. 'I'm so sorry.'

'It's okay. I'm not alone after all.' Sebastian then pointed up at the sky. 'I know that mum is up there watching me and that she is proud of having me as her son.'

Kate was nearly brought to tears by Sebastian's words. She knew that her friend's mother was dead but even in death, she was probably smiling and protecting her son like a guardian angel. Still, she was happy that Sebastian's mother was still with him in his heart, unlike her own selfish mother, who was disgusted to have a daughter like Kate all because she had autism.

'Are you okay?' Sebastian asked his friend.

'Y-yeah,' Kate replied. 'I just thought life would be hard for you and Jake without your mother.'

'Not really. Dad said if I ever get sad, I look up to the sky and talk to mum.'

Kate lowered her head.

Sebastian got up from his chair and sat down beside Kate. 'Are you sure that you're alright?'

Kate let out a soft sigh and then looked at her friend. 'We've been friends since we were kids, right?'

'Yeah.'

'You know I accept you as my friend and not by your disability, right?'

'Yes. And I accepted you as my friend because you care about me.'

Kate turned away from Sebastian.

'Is something wrong?'

'I found out yesterday from Uncle Samuel that I live in the same world as you,' she said, looking back at Sebastian.

'What does that mean?'

'It means that I have...autism.'

Sebastian instantly jumped to his feet. 'You're kidding me, right?'

Kate shook her head.

'Oh my gosh,' he said as he walked to the edge of the pool.

Dammit brain! Kate thought. *I blame you for opening my mouth.*

Sebastian took a deep breath and then sat back down beside Kate. 'I thought you were just a normal girl who loves art.'

'I thought so too until yesterday.'

'How did you find out that you're autistic?'

'It's a long story and I'd rather not speak of it.'

Sebastian looked away from Kate.

Great! Kate thought. *Now that he knows the truth, he'll probably doesn't want to be friends with me.*

'Look, if you don't want to be friends with me anymore, I'll understand.'

'What are you talking about?' said Sebastian, looking back at Kate.

'Now that you know the truth, you'll probably want to be friends with someone who is normal.'

'Why would I end our friendship now that I know that you're autistic?'

'Because I'm not normal anymore?'

Sebastian shook his head. 'We are normal but in a different way.'

'What do you mean by that?'

'Well, I love video games and wrestling, right?'

Kate nodded her head.

'And you love art, right?'

Kate nodded her head again.

'When you paint, you see a different world, am I right?'

'Yes.'

'And when I play video games, I see something more than a bunch of code put together to create a game. I take the time to learn about colour, text, et cetera.'

'How does that make us normal?'

'Just because we're on the spectrum doesn't make us less human.'

'I...I guess you're right.'

Sebastian stood up. 'I'm going to see if dad's done talking with Samuel.'

With that, Sebastian walked back inside the house, leaving Kate alone.

Kate looked back at the ocean for a moment and then got up and followed Sebastian.

Inside, she saw the two adults talking to Sebastian. She quietly walked up to Samuel without interrupting their conversation.

'Oh, here she is,' said Samuel, noticing Kate beside him.

He wrapped his arm around Kate and rubbed the side of her arm.

'Say, dad, did you know that Kate is autistic just like me?' Sebastian said to his father.

Jake turned his attention to Samuel. 'So, she knows now.'

'I had to,' Samuel responded.

'Wait! What?' Kate said to Samuel with confusion. 'Jake already knew that I'm autistic?'

'I didn't know what to do once I got your diagnosis. I had to ask Jake for some advice.'

Kate pulled Samuel's arm off her. 'Does anyone else know about my condition?'

'The museum employees,' Jake answered.

'Ahem!' Samuel said to Jake.

'Sorry, boss.'

'Look, I know that you're worried about people finding out that you're autistic, but the truth is, you're not alone,' Samuel explained to Kate. 'After all, there are plenty of people in the world that have autism. I mean, look at Jake. He's also part of the crowd.'

Kate instantly looked at Jake with her jaw open.

Jake slowly nodded.

'I...I thought you were normal.'

'I might be like you and Sebastian but I'm still Jake after all,' Jake replied. 'I did not let my disability stop me from getting a job and raising Sebastian.'

Kate closed her mouth and went to the dinner table and sat down with her head lowered.

'Is she alright?' Sebastian asked Samuel.

'She'll be fine,' Samuel answered. 'Just go and have some fun with your father.'

'Are you sure, boss?' Jake questioned his friend.

'I'm sure.'

Jake and Sebastian said their goodbyes to Kate before they left the house, but she paid no attention to them.

Samuel walked over to Kate and sat down beside her. He went to place his hand on her shoulder only for her to pull away.

'Don't touch me!' Kate demanded.

'What's wrong, Honey Dragon?'

'I'm confused! That's what's wrong.'

'With that?'

'This whole autism thingy. I mean, look at Jake. I thought he was normal.'

She then dropped her head in her arms on the table.

Samuel looked away from Kate for a moment and then he let out a soft sigh. 'There's something I need to show you tomorrow.'

'I don't want to go anywhere tomorrow.'

'No, trust me, you'll like it.'

Kate lifted her head. 'Fine.'

'Excellent!' Samuel said with a smile. 'Make sure you bring your diary.'

'Why?'

'You'll see.'

With that, Samuel went upstairs to his room.

What did he mean by that? Kate thought, puzzled.

She went to her bedroom and played her music while she lay on her bed and looked up at her zodiac animal.

Am I no longer able to follow my zodiac sign now that I'm autistic? Kate thought and then closed her eyes.

'Kate?' said Samuel. 'Wake up, Honey Dragon.'

Kate opened her eyes and saw Samuel sitting on the side of her bed. 'Oh, hi uncle.'

'Are you okay now?'

'Not really,' she said as she sat up. 'I'm still confused.'

Samuel went to Kate's table and grabbed the plate of sandwiches he made and took them over to Kate.

'Have a bite,' he said as he handed Kate the plate before sitting back down.

Kate instantly dug her teeth into a sandwich.

'I know it's a lot to take in about your disorder but trust me, you'll get used to it in no time,' said Samuel. 'It's like riding a bike.'

'Yeah, except the bike has one wheel instead of two.'

'Honey Dragon.'

'I mean, how did I even get autism in the first place?'

'It's a genetic thing, I'm afraid.'

'What?' she mumbled while chewing.

'You see, when I was adopted into your father's family, he had…well… anger issues. He never got checked out as my adoptive parents thought he was just a normal kid who didn't listen to his parents.'

'What does that have to do with autism being passed onto me?'

'I reckon that if your father had got checked out, things would've been different – instead of me finding out later that you have your father's "special" gene.'

Kate ate her sandwich until there was nothing but crumbs on the plate, and then Samuel took the empty plate downstairs.

Kate got up and turned off her music before lying back down on her bed. She looked up at her zodiac animal.

'Genetic,' said Kate. 'Why couldn't I just inherit genes from Samuel instead of dad?'

Kate slapped her forehead. 'I forgot. He was adopted.' She sighed. 'The only thing I got from mum was her beauty.'

I wish that I was Samuel's daughter. Maybe then, I would be normal just like him. Kate took a deep breath. *But no! I'm stuck with broken genes from someone who I have never seen in my life.*

She grabbed her stuffed panda and placed it on her chest while she stroked her fingers through its fur.

'Whatever Samuel is planning on showing me tomorrow, it will probably be a waste of time.'

Kate let out a soft sigh and then closed her eyes.

I better just play along until I get bored.

Chapter 20

Early the next morning, Kate got up and got dressed. She brushed her hair before tying it up.

Whatever Samuel needs to show me, it better be quick, Kate grumbled as she looked at herself in the bathroom mirror.

She lowered her head as she walked out of her room and went across the bridge into her studio. She grabbed her diary and her pencil case and then walked downstairs to find Samuel pouring cereal into bowls before adding milk. Kate quietly placed her diary and pencil case on the dinner table before sitting down with her head down.

Samuel saw Kate quiet as a little sparrow. He put the milk and the cereal away before he brought the bowls to the dinner table.

'Morning, Honey Dragon,' he smiled as he placed the bowls down and sat beside Kate.

Kate said nothing as she grabbed her spoon and began to eat her breakfast.

Samuel's smile quickly disappeared. He ate his breakfast while ignoring the silence that surrounded the house.

'What a beautiful day for a drive,' he said, midway through his breakfast.

Kate paid no attention to Samuel. Samuel closed his mouth.

When the pair was done eating, Samuel took the dirty bowls to the sink while Kate remained quiet at the dinner table.

'Do you want to get ready while I'm cleaning up?' Samuel asked Kate.

Kate said nothing. She grabbed her diary and pencil case, went into the garage and placed her items into the car. She then returned to her room, grabbed her phone and then went back downstairs and got into the car. She sat in total silence for a solid twenty minutes with her head down until she spotted Samuel out of the corner of her eye. She watched him walking past her window with a towel rolled up.

Samuel placed the towel into the boot and then went to grab his wallet and keys before getting into the car.

'Ready?' said Samuel.

'No,' Kate answered and then turned her attention to the window.

Samuel was about to ask Kate what was bothering her, but instead, he closed his mouth and drove out of the garage and onto the highway.

Kate quietly watched her feathered friends as they flew past her like tiny rockets. *If I was a real hummingbird, I wouldn't have to worry about being different.* She then let out a sad sigh. *Unfortunately, I'm stuck with a strange body with an abnormal brain.*

'Hey,' said Samuel. 'Do you want to play your music? I don't mind listening to your favourite artist.'

'No,' Kate answered.

'Come on! Playing your music always make you happy.'

'I said no!' she roared at Samuel.

Samuel instantly went quiet.

'I-I'm sorry uncle. I'm just confused and broken.'

'Broken? Whoever said that you're broken?'

'Mum.'

Samuel shook his head. 'Well, your mother is not here to bother us anymore, remember?'

'I know, but...'

'But nothing. She's the broken one, not you.'

'Yeah right. You won't say the word because you're my uncle.'

'An uncle who has raised you since you were a baby. Unlike your selfish mother, I used my time to raise you with love and support. Did I ever treat you differently? Nope. I never once thought that you were broken. In fact, you surprised me when you were a kid.'

'How did I surprise you?'

'While most other kids would scribble, you were able to draw people and items realistically.'

'I did?'

'Yeah, your special brain helped you achieve your talent for art.'

'Special brain? What does that mean?'

'I'll tell you once we get to the spot.'

Kate looked back at the window and continued to watch her feathered friends.

Two hours later, they parked the car near the gentle river alongside the other cars. The tall thin trees waved their leaves in the wind from across the river.

Kate got out of the car with her diary and pencil case in her arms and watched the river quietly running past, while her friends flew over her head and into the clouds. She lowered her head as she walked back to Samuel, who was taking the towel out from the back of the car.

'Where are we?' Kate asked as she lifted her head.

'Follow me and you'll find out,' Samuel answered. He closed the boot and then locked his car.

Kate grumbled under her breath as she followed Samuel through a jungle full of thin tall trees.

'It's such a wonderful day to come out here and wander through nature,' said Samuel.

'Wow,' Kate mumbled as she looked at the gravel road underneath her feet.

'It would be a lot better if you look up.'

Kate looked up at the trees for a moment and then looked back down at the ground.

'Come on! Where's the artist that I know.'

'She's gone. Just like the creative world.'

'I don't believe you.'

'Look, just tell me why we're here so that we can go home.'

'You'll see.'

Kate wouldn't look up. She just continued grumbling through the maze of trees for another twelve minutes.

I want to go home she complained right before she bumped into Samuel. 'Hey! Why did you stop in the middle of the road?'

'We're here,' said Samuel.

Kate looked up and was instantly amazed.

Standing in the middle of the jungle was a gargantuan tree with massive roots that grew into the ground. Its branches blocked out the sun like an umbrella with its green, healthy leaves.

'What is this place?' Kate asked Samuel.

'This place is called the Soundless Forest,' Samuel answered as he rolled out the towel and then sat down on it. 'As for the tree, it is called the Wonderous Tree.'

'Why is it called that?'

'People would come here and gaze at the tree's magnificent beauty while enjoying the peaceful forest.'

Kate sat down beside Samuel while her eyes remained fixed on the tree's stunning beauty. 'It's...it's beautiful,' she said as he placed her diary and pencil case on the towel.

'It's more than a beautiful tree. People would often visit the tree and would leave the place with a smile on their face.'

Kate couldn't take her eyes off the tree. There was something mystical about it that she couldn't explain.

She had seen many beautiful trees around the world with Samuel whenever they went on holidays. She would often draw them in her diary, but the gigantic tree that stood proudly in the middle of all the other trees, was something she could only imagine in her creative world.

'How did you find this place?' Kate asked, looking at Samuel.

'When I came to Night Valley, my adoptive parents brought me and James here to show me that they weren't scary and that they will forever love me as one of their own. And so that James and I would get along as brothers.'

'Did the tree help?'

'I felt safe with my adoptive parents but not with James.'

'What happened with dad?'

'He had a tantrum and nearly punched me in the stomach.'

'Ouch!'

'Luckily my adoptive parents managed to get him to calm down.'

'That must be tough having to deal with dad's outbursts.'

Samuel shook his head. 'You had no idea. Sometimes when he would have an outburst, he would threaten to kill me.'

Kate covered her mouth in shock. 'Did you say something to your parents?'

'I did. I said that something was wrong with James and that he should get checked out.'

'What did they say?'

'They said to ignore James and that he'd eventually grow out of his tantrums.'

'Did he?'

'Of course not. When you have undiagnosed autism, you tend to lash out in anger.'

Samuel then lowered his head. 'When I was your age, James got so angry one day that we got into a fight, and I accidentally punched several of his teeth out.'

Kate's eyes widened in shock. 'Did you do it on purpose?'

'I did it in self-defence.'

'What did your parents do?'

'They told me to get out of the house.'

'Wait...what?'

Samuel nodded his head. 'Yup. They told me to get out of the house because I was hurting their son. I tried explaining to them, but they didn't believe me and tossed me out in the rain.'

'What happened after that?'

'I went to Jake's house. You see, we've been friends since high school.'

Kate nodded her head.

'I told Jake and his parents everything and they took me in as one of their own until I finished high school. They even helped me get into university.'

That's when Kate spotted the tears in Samuel's eyes. 'I promised to help Jake's parents with their retirement after I graduated from university.'

'And did you?' said Kate.

'Yup. I gave them enough money to travel around the world as a thank you for raising me and helping me with my schooling.'

'Are they still travelling?'

Samuel nodded his head. 'They occasionally stop by and visit the museum while you and Sebastian are at school and say hi to me and Jake.'

'Can I see Sebastian's grandparents one day?'

'Of course. Once they're not travelling.'

'So, may I ask what happened in the end with your adoptive parents?'

Samuel wiped the teardrops from his eyes with his hand. 'Well, one day while I was busy doing paperwork in my office, they decided to visit me.'

'Oh no.'

'Oh no indeed. They walked into my office pretending that they were happy to see me again and that they were thankful to have raised a successful son.'

'Excuse me?'

'Exactly the words that I said to them.'

Kate shook her head as she crossed her arms. 'Unbelievable. Why would they come back to you once you'd become successful?'

'They only came back because I was making good money. If I'd had a normal job, they wouldn't have come back.'

Of course, Kate thought. 'What happened?'

'They told me their sob story. They said that James ran away with all their money and that they were about to be homeless unless I helped them out by giving them money.'

Kate rolled her eyes with annoyance while Samuel shook his head.

'Did you help them?' Kate replied.

'Of course not! They abandoned me when I was fifteen. Why should I help them?'

'So, what did you do?'

'I said goodbye and I kicked them out of my museum.'

'Did they ever come back?'

'Oh, yes. They kept coming back and kept demanding that I give them money or else they'd sue me.'

Kate slapped her forehead with her hand. 'Please tell me they went to jail.'

'They did. They were charged with extortion and my lawyer made sure that they stayed behind bars.'

What a relief. Kate then changed the subject. 'Going back to your story, how did you find out that Jake was autistic?'

'One day while I was doing homework, I saw that Jake was getting frustrated with his homework and I thought that he was going to burst out in anger. So, I went to find his parents and told them that something was wrong with Jake. They sat down with me and explained to me that he has ADHD and reassured me that I was safe.'

'Is that what Sebastian has?'

Samuel nodded his head.

'Did Jake ever hurt you?'

'Nope. Unlike your father, Jake learnt to control his anger.'

'Why didn't he tell me that he was on the spectrum?'

'Because he doesn't need to tell everyone that he has autism.'

Kate turned her head away from Samuel.

Samuel grabbed Kate's diary and pencil case and placed them on her knee, making her look back at him.

'I want you to draw me something,' he said.

'Like what?'

'I want you to draw me what you think autism looks like.'

Kate took out her pencil from her case and began to sketch in her diary.

After about half an hour of constant drawing, Kate placed her pencil down and then handed Samuel her diary.

Samuel looked at the two sketches. One of them was a hammerhead shark showing its razor-sharp teeth with the word: "scary" written underneath. The other picture was a maze with a person standing at the entrance with the word: "confusing" written underneath.

'Okay...' he said as he turned to a new page. 'Can I use your pencil?'

Kate handed it to Samuel.

She watched him draw a funny stick person with two lines on its head, which was supposed to be the hair. She burst out into laughter when she saw what appeared to be a penguin floating in the middle of the page with a peacock's tail.

'What is that supposed to be?' she laughed.

'It's a hummingbird,' Samuel answered.

'It looks like a penguin trying to fly.'

'It's a hummingbird. Come on! You know I'm not an artist like you.'

Kate fell back onto the towel from the extreme laughter while tears poured out from her eyes.

'I'll just wait until you're done laughing.'

About five minutes later, Kate sat up and then wiped her tears from her eyes.

'As I was saying before you laughed like one of your feathered friends, this is a hummingbird,' said Samuel.

'Penguin,' Kate replied.

Samuel ignored Kate. 'This is your nickname animal.'

'Penguin,' she giggled.

'If you say penguin again, I'm just going to ignore you.'

Kate said nothing while she tried to contain her giggles.

'As I was saying, this hummingbird represents your personality, talent and your special heart.'

'How?'

'Remember how I said that a fragile but strong hummingbird had been born inside you?'

'Yeah.'

'What if I told you that little bird is your friend.'

'It is?'

'Yeah! The pictures you drew of what autism looks like to you, it's not about fear and confusion.'

'But it is! And I don't know if I'll ever fit in the crowd.'

Samuel pointed at the hummingbird. 'Autism is this little guy right here.'

'The hummingbird?'

'Yes,' he said and then pointed at the stick person. 'The tiny bird is the reason why you can draw and paint pictures that tell a story without having to open your mouth.'

'But...but autism is supposed to be confusing and fearful.'

'Autism is not confusing and fearful. In fact, I heard that some people are thankful to be on the spectrum.'

'They are?'

'Remember how I would hold events at the museum to raise money for people in need and to spread awareness?'

'The boring speech presentations that I always slept through as a kid?'

'Yes. Well, if you had paid attention all those years ago, you would've learnt from the guest speakers that without their special gift, they wouldn't have been able to achieve their dream.'

'All except for me,' she said, looking away.

Samuel placed the diary and pencil down. 'Look at me, Honey Dragon.'

Kate slowly looked back at Samuel.

'Have you ever thought that you could use autism to your advantage?' he asked.

'How?'

'Well, instead of having one fantasy world with hundreds of thoughts wanting to be painted, you could have a thousand fantasy worlds with thousands of thoughts wanting to be painted.'

Kate's eyebrow rose with confusion.

Samuel handed Kate her diary and pencil. He then pointed at the tree.

'Look,' he said. 'I see a normal tree but what do you see.'

'I see–'

'Don't tell me, draw what you see. Use that creative brain of yours.'

Kate looked at the tree for a minute and then began to sketch while Samuel gazed at the tree and its many branches.

She would sometimes stop to look back up the tree. She would even work with her coloured pencils.

An hour later, Kate handed Samuel her diary.

'My goodness,' said Samuel with surprise.

The tree that Kate had drawn had colourful butterflies flying around it like fireflies. There were a couple of foxes sitting on the grass, watching the tree.

'Is the picture horrible?' Kate asked.

'This...this picture is amazing,' Samuel replied. 'I don't have the imagination or the skills to draw something so mystical.'

'That's why you're a history professor and not an artist,' she said as she put her pencils back into her pencil case.

'But you just showed me that you can use autism to your advantage.'

'No, I didn't.'

'Yes, you did. And that's why you drew this picture with whatever emotion you were feeling and expressed it through drawing.'

Kate still didn't believe her uncle. She had always used emotion whenever she painted and drew. 'I'm sorry, uncle, but I still don't believe that I've used autism to my advantage.'

Samuel thought for a moment as he closed Kate's diary and handed it back to her. 'I have another place that I want to show you.'

'If it's another giant tree, forget it.'

'No, trust me. It will make things clearer for you.'

'Fine.'

They returned to the car. Kate put her art materials down and instantly looked out the window as soon as she got into the passenger seat. Samuel dumped the towel into the boot of the car, got into his seat and drove off.

A couple of hours later, the pair parked near the other cars on the side of the road before getting out and walking along the concrete footpath through the field of grass with endless numbers of trees growing on it.

'So, what's this place?' Kate asked Samuel.

'The Calm Gardens,' Samuel answered. 'I brought you here the day after your mother left you on my doorstep and while I was young and handsome.'

'You still are. You have women still trying to win your heart.'

'That's funny. I remember someone calling me an old man.'

'I'm so sorry, uncle. I was just angry.'

'I know. It was my fault for not telling you the truth sooner.'

'Did you ever get women approach you when they saw you with me?'

'Yup. Many times.'

'Did they say anything?'

'They all thought that you were my daughter.'

'Seriously?'

'I know. I had to keep explaining to them that you were my niece.'

He then shook his head. 'Some of them got excited and thought they had a chance to get close to me so that they could have children with me.'

'So, what happened?'

'We ended up going home in the end. I couldn't enjoy my walk without women trying to get close to me.'

Kate glanced around and saw a crowd of people enjoying watching the trees. Some of them happily jogged along the footpath while they listened to music through their headphones.

'Let's just hope the ladies don't interrupt us while we're walking,' she said.

'Pay no attention to them,' Samuel responded. 'If you don't make eye contact, they won't bother us.'

'Yes, uncle.'

The pair continued walking until they saw a tree that had pink flowers blossoming in the sun.

'There it is,' said Samuel as he approached it.

'We came all this way just to find a pink tree?' said Kate as she followed Samuel.

Samuel ignored Kate as he looked at the flowers.

'Hello,' said Kate as she waved her hand in front of Samuel's face.

Yet again, Samuel ignored Kate.

Kate poked Samuel's shoulder until she gained his attention. 'Why did we come to see a pink tree?'

'Look at the flowers,' said Samuel. 'Tell me if you see anything different.'

Kate looked up at the flowers. Every branch had beautiful pink flowers. She took a step closer to the tree and spotted a branch that had one purple flower blossoming next to the other flowers.

'A purple flower among the pink flowers,' she said, looking at Samuel.

'That's it,' Samuel replied.

'What is a purple flower doing among the pink flowers?'

'And what's wrong with the purple flower?'

'It doesn't look right. I mean, every flower on this tree is pink.'

'There's nothing wrong with the flower. It's how it blossomed that makes it unique.'

Kate shook her head, but more with uncertainty than disbelief this time. 'No, it doesn't. It looks odd.'

'Being odd is what makes it stand out.'

Does it? She tried to see it the way Samuel did, but it was hard.

'All these flowers chose to be pink because they were told so. Except for one flower. It didn't want to be pink, so it became purple.'

'But why, though?'

'It chose to stand out from the crowd. Just like those who have a disability.'

'Really?'

Samuel nodded his head. 'Look at Sebastian for an example. He might be a famous gamer or a famous video game maker in the future. Who knows?' He then placed his hand onto Kate's shoulder. 'Or you. A famous artist one day.'

Kate pushed Samuel's hand off her shoulder. 'How can I be an artist when I have autism? I'll never be like the other artists in the world.'

'Why would you want to be the same when you can be different?'

'What do you mean by that?'

'I mean, why do you want to be a pink flower and not a purple flower?'

Kate looked away from Samuel. 'I...I don't know.'

Samuel pulled out the hummingbird necklace that he had given to Kate from his pocket and placed it around her neck.

'You were born to be unique,' he said. 'Even with your disability, you're still a unique person.'

Kate looked at the hummingbird for a moment and then looked up at Samuel. She was about to open her mouth when Samuel stopped her from speaking.

'If you're going to talk about autism being bad, don't say it,' he said.

'But...'

'No but's. Forget about the negative words about autism and think of positive words like creative and curious.'

Kate looked back up at the purple flower for a moment and then back at Samuel with a smile on her face. 'I...I guess you're right.'

'See! Being autistic is not a bad thing. It's a part of your heart after all, and you should be thankful that you have the special gift.'

Kate tightly wrapped her arms around Samuel and rested her head on his chest. 'You're right, uncle. Thank you for opening my eyes and helping me understand autism a bit better.'

Samuel hugged Kate. 'I'm thankful to have such a talented and beautiful niece like you in my life.'

'And I'm thankful to be raised by a man who didn't abandon me just because I'm on the spectrum.'

Their hug was interrupted by the sound of a woman's voice.

'It's Professor Wood!' the woman squealed with excitement.

'That's our exit cue,' said Samuel, and he and Kate sprinted back to the car.

Samuel drove off right before the crowd of women could get close to touching his car.

'That was too close,' said Kate.

'I know,' Samuel replied.

'Do you think that women will ever stop chasing you?'

'Maybe when I'm old and weak perhaps then I'll have some peace. Until then, nope.'

I hope so.

Back at the house, Kate went upstairs to her studio. She grabbed a blank canvas and placed it on her easel. She sat and stared at the canvas for a while until she felt a hand on her shoulder. She turned her head and saw Samuel standing behind her.

'Are you okay now?' Samuel asked Kate.

'Yeah,' Kate answered.

'You know you can talk to me if you ever feel scared or confused.'

'I know, I know.'

Samuel turned his attention towards the blank canvas. 'What are you going to paint?'

'I'll show you tomorrow. For now, could you kindly leave my studio?'

'As you wish, Miss Artist.' With that, he left.

Kate looked at her necklace for a moment and then grabbed her pencil and began to sketch. She would occasionally stop to use her eraser and then go back to drawing her picture.

After a while of drawing, Kate was satisfied with the outline. She placed her pencil on the table and grabbed her paintbrush and paint.

'This is it, brain,' said Kate. 'Do your magic.'

Kate dipped her paintbrush into the paint and began to add colour to her painting.

Several hours later, Kate left her studio with a smile on her face. She went into her bathroom and took a hot shower and then changed into her pyjamas.

She then went downstairs to find Samuel cooking pasta. Kate quietly walked up beside Samuel and grabbed the plates from the cupboard.

'There she is,' said Samuel as he turned his head to Kate. 'How's the painting going?'

'It's coming along well,' said Kate as she placed the plates on the bench. 'I just need to add more details and colour to it, and it should be done by tomorrow.'

'Can I at least know what you're painting?'

'No.'

'Is it an animal?'

'I ain't telling you anything until you see it for yourself tomorrow.'

'Of course,' he smiled.

Kate filled some cups with water before putting them on the table, then finished setting the table with cutlery. She then sat down and waited patiently for Samuel to finish cooking.

After ten minutes, Samuel served the pasta and sat beside Kate. The two of them grabbed their forks and began to eat their dinner.

'Mmm...this tastes so good,' said Kate.

'Oh, really? I thought you preferred your mother's chefs' cooking,' said Samuel.

'I did like their cooking, but I prefer your meals. They are simple and filled with love.'

Samuel smiled as he and Kate went back to eating pasta.

'Although...' Kate said.

'What?' Samuel replied.

'Can we hire a chef just for one day?'

Samuel raised his eyebrow.

'Just kidding!' Kate laughed, making Samuel slap his forehead.

After dinner, they took their dishes to the sink.

'Hey, uncle,' said Kate as she watched Samuel clean the dishes.

'Yes, Kate?' Samuel replied.

'I know this might sound a bit personal but, is this the reason why you didn't give up on me?'

'Excuse me?'

'I mean, you were left at an orphanage as a kid, and you were abandoned by your adoptive parents. Is that why you decide to keep me?'

Samuel looked away from Kate.

'Uncle?'

'Life wasn't perfect for me growing up,' Samuel responded, looking back at Kate. 'As a kid, I only wished to be a parent. I didn't care if I had a job or not. I just wanted to be a parent.'

'Oh.'

'When your mother cheated on me with James, I thought I would never be a parent. However, when she was pregnant, I thought this was finally my chance. If I couldn't be a father, I could be an uncle instead.'

'That must've broken your heart.'

'At the beginning, yes. But the moment you were brought into this world, I was finally an uncle.' Samuel drained the water and then dried his hands. 'The moment I told your mother about your diagnosis, she chose to leave you in the dark while I chose to keep you as my niece.'

Oh.

'That's why I raised you alone. I didn't want to see an innocent soul like you trying to survive in this world without a parental figure.'

Tears slowly poured down Kate's face.

Samuel gently wiped the teardrops from her face with his thumb.

Kate wrapped her arms around Samuel and let her teardrops soak his shirt. 'I'm so happy that I have you in my life.'

'And I'm happy to have you in *my* life,' Samuel replied as he wrapped his arms around Kate and patted her back.

After a couple of minutes, Kate freed herself from Samuel's grasp and wiped her tears with her hand.

'Are you going to tell me what you're painting?' Samuel asked Kate.

'No,' Kate answered.

'Whatever you say, Miss Artist.'

Kate rolled her eyes as she went upstairs, leaving Samuel alone in the kitchen.

Samuel smiled and then looked at his drenched shirt. 'Thanks for the wet present, Kate.'

He shook his head and then went back to cleaning the kitchen.

Kate stood beside her bedroom window and looked up at the glowing crescent moon that shone brighter in the night sky.

'This is it,' she said. 'I hope Uncle Samuel will like this painting better than the other ones that I've done.'

And to show him that I have used autism to my advantage.

Chapter 21

Early the next morning, Kate dragged her half-asleep body down the stairs to find Samuel in the kitchen dressed in his gym clothes and putting his protein shake and healthy snack bars into his gym bag.

'Where are you off to?' Kate asked Samuel.

'Where do you think I'm going?'

'To work.'

Samuel looked at Kate with his eyebrow raised.

'I'm just kidding,' Kate giggled as she walked up to him. 'I know you're going to the gym.'

'I'll probably be gone for a few hours,' he said as he placed his gym bag over his shoulder.

'That's okay. I'll just be painting in my studio.'

Samuel nodded his head. 'Call me if you have any problems.'

'I know, uncle,' she grumbled.

'Okay,' he said. He grabbed his keys and wallet. 'I'll see you in a couple of hours.'

With that, Samuel walked into the garage.

Kate made and ate her breakfast in total silence.

Once she was done, she left the bowl soaking and returned to her bedroom. She dressed, grabbed her phone and went to her studio and closed the door.

She started her favourite artist playlist on her phone and then grabbed her paintbrush and continued painting whilst listening to the fantasy-like, energetic melody that played in the background.

Her song list would go from happy to sad, motivating to peacefulness. There are even songs that create a fantasy world thanks to the beautiful angel who sang the heavenly lyrics for most of the songs. She would often play her favourite artist for hours and would never get sick of listening to the songs.

After a couple of hours, Kate placed her paintbrush and paint down on the table. She then stopped her music, rose from her chair and took a step back.

She smiled at her finished painting – a hummingbird with brightly coloured wings, drinking nectar from a flower.

'This painting better leave Samuel speechless,' she said. 'If he doesn't, then I give up with that man.'

She walked out of her studio and closed the door behind her and then went downstairs only to find Samuel walking out of the garage with his headphones covering his ears. His shirt was covered with unpleasant sweat marks.

'You're back, uncle,' said Kate.

Samuel ignored Kate as he placed his bag on the kitchen bench.

'Uncle,' she said as she waved her hand in front of Samuel's face.

'Huh?' said Samuel as he took off his headphones.

'I said you're back.'

'Oh, yes.'

'And of course, you smell,' she said while pinching her nose with two fingers.

Samuel shook his head as he placed his phone on the dinner table along with his headphones.

'How's the painting going?' he asked as he took off his shoes and socks.

'It's done,' Kate answered.

'Can I see it?'

'Maybe once you smell like a flower, then I'll let you look.'

Samuel shook his head as he walked out into the backyard with Kate following from behind.

She sat down on the pool chair and watched Samuel as he took his shirt off and dumped it on the ground and then jumped into the pool.

He may not smell like a flower but at least he won't smell like a skunk, Kate thought as Samuel came up to the surface and flicked his hair back. 'How's the water?'

'It's nice,' Samuel answered. 'You should join me.'

'Maybe later.'

'Of course.'

Samuel swam laps for several minutes, cleaning off the sweat. Once he was done, he got out of the pool and wrapped the towel around his waist and then sat down on the pool chair next to Kate.

'That's better,' he said. 'At least now I don't smell.'

'Yeah, you just need to wear deodorant to cover up your chlorine odour,' Kate replied.

'I will. Don't you worry.'

Once Samuel was dry, he went to his bedroom to change while Kate sat the dinner table and waited patiently.

A couple of minutes later, Samuel walked downstairs, grabbed his smelly socks and put them in the washing machine and then placed his shoes near the front door. He then unpacked his bag. After that, he took his phone and headphones to his room with Kate following from behind.

'So,' said Samuel as he placed the items onto his bedside table. 'Can I see the painting now?'

'Yes, but you have to close your eyes,' Kate replied.

'Fine,' he said. He closed his eyes and then covered them with his hand.

Kate took Samuel's other hand and carefully guided him out of his room and across the bridge. She used her free hand to open the studio door and then pulled him into the room before releasing his hand.

'Okay,' she said. 'You can open your eyes.'

Samuel lowered his hand and then opened his eyes.

'My goodness,' he said in an awestruck whisper.

'So, what do you think?' Kate asked.

'It's beautiful. In fact, I love this painting more than all your other paintings and drawings.'

'Hey!'

'I mean it in a good way.'

'Sure, you do.'

'No, I mean it. How did you even come up with such an inspiration?'

'Well, I did what you said to me yesterday. You said to use autism to my advantage. So, I did.'

Samuel wrapped his arm around Kate. 'That's my girl.' He then looked back at the painting. 'I think this painting should be hanging up in an art gallery.'

'Really?' Kate said with excitement.

'Yup. In fact, if you keep painting and sell a lot of paintings, you could have your own art gallery one day just like me owning a museum.'

Kate spent a moment imagining people from all over the world visiting her art gallery and witnessing her world of art. She even imagined herself being famous just like her uncle.

'You're right,' said Kate. 'Maybe when I become a famous artist, I'll have my own Porsche or even a Lamborghini.'

Samuel turned his attention to Kate. 'Being famous is no easy step, you know that.'

'I know.'

'You've got to keep working hard if you want to mark your name in history.'

Kate nodded her head.

Samuel released Kate from his grasp and then turned to face her.

'I just want to warn you now that in the future when you become an artist, there will be people out there that will try and drag you down.'

'Like Mary for example,' Kate pointed out.

'That's only one person. There will be thousands of people who will try to stop you from achieving your dream.'

'Did you ever have people trying to drag you down?'

'Oh, yes. Plenty. They all thought that my dream of owning a museum was worthless and that I would never make it.'

'Well, you definitely proved them wrong.'

'Yup. I ignored those haters and continued to follow my passion for history and well, look at me now. I am a famous history professor and a museum owner.'

'And a woman magnet.'

'Kate!'

'Just kidding,' she giggled.

Samuel shook his head and then turned back to the painting.

Kate stepped up beside Samuel and stared at it with him.

For several minutes, the pair said nothing as they looked at the painting until Kate broke the ice.

'If I do become a famous artist one day, do you think that guys will chase after me?'

'Oh, they definitely will chase after you for your money.'

'Right. I almost forgot about that.'

'If you ever want to find your soulmate one day, make sure that he loves you for your personality and not by how much money you have.'

'Yes, uncle.'

'If a guy starts asking you for expensive gifts like a car, dump him immediately.'

'Sounds a bit harsh but okay. Anything else that I need to watch out for?'

'I'll tell you one day when you start going out with guys.'

Kate nodded her head and then changed the subject. 'Hey uncle.'

'Yes?'

'I just want to say thank you for helping me understand about autism and that it isn't a bad thing after all.'

'Anytime, Kate.'

'If I ever become a famous artist, I want to show other people who have a disability that they can still achieve their dream.'

'I reckon that you'll be a great inspiration.'

'You think so?'

'Of course!' he said, right before Kate wrapped her arms around him.

'Thank you for believing in me. I love you, uncle.'

'And I love you too, Honey Dragon.'

Acknowledgements

I would like to thank the wonderful, beautiful editor Narrelle Harris for helping me write this wonderful book.

I also want to thank my mum and my brother for supporting my dream of being a writer even when I buy hundreds of notebooks and pens and would rather listen to music and write whenever we go on vacations instead of socialising with the family.

About Ashlie Parfitt

Ashlie Parfitt was born and raised in sunny Queensland, where she's lived for her entire life. As a kid, she was always shy and quiet.

Her world changed the day when she was diagnosed with Asperger's Syndrome at age fifteen.

She fell in love with writing during high school but didn't write Honey Dragon until she graduated.

She also found that writing helped her communicate her thoughts and emotions through storytelling.

When she's writing (or not writing), she often listens to Two Steps from Hell and Thomas Bergersen and annoys her family with her favourite music to the point that they ask her to turn it off. She also enjoys playing video games.